The Mystery of The Missing Buddha

The Mystery of The Missing Buddha

A Singh Sisters' Adventure

Maulshree Mahajan

PARTRIDGE
A Penguin Random House Company

ISBN:	Hardcover	978-1-4828-2146-8
	Softcover	978-1-4828-2145-1
	eBook	978-1-4828-2144-4

To order additional copies of this book, contact
Partridge India
000 800 10062 62
orders.india@partridgepublishing.com

www.partridgepublishing.com/india

Dedication

Dedicated to my parents, Usha Mahajan and Prof. Joginder Kumar Gupta, who encourage me to dream, work hard and achieve. I am who I am because of them.

ACKNOWLEDGEMENTS

My heartfelt thanks to:

My husband Girish, whose support has given me the freedom to discover and reinvent myself.

My sister Tanushree, the first reader of the initial draft, who gave me her feedback in the middle of the night saying, "Finish it in two days, I want to know what happens next." It gave me the confidence I needed at the time.

My parents, who have been the driving force behind my persistence to pursue my passions.

My extended family, which includes my friends and cousins who have, through the years, heard and appreciated my stories.

My friends, who consistently encourage me to keep writing, and have always been there for me.

My students, who make me believe that I am on the right path.

Partridge India Publishing—A Penguin Random House Company, for having faith in me and my story.

Ms. Abha Iyengar, for patiently editing the manuscript.

CONTENTS

CHAPTER 1

The Singh Sisters' Journey on Their Own

Tara's dark-brown eyes were glued to the bus window for almost an hour now. She was taking in the scenic beauty abundantly scattered outside . . . the beautiful *deodar* trees, streams meandering lazily on the mountains, the lush greenery and the colourful flowers, and most of all, the mildly-scented, cool, pollution free air.

Fourteen year old Tara lived in New Delhi with her parents and her twin sister Meera. Meera was, at present, busy reading a teen mystery book. Although Meera and Tara were twins, they did not look alike; in fact their interests and attitudes were also very different. Both of them were very slim and tall for their age, but the similarities ended there.

Tara generally dressed and behaved as though she was a little princess. She loved watching television, helping her mom in the kitchen and admiring herself in the mirror. She wore a long black skirt with a pink, floral-printed blouse that day. Her straight, black, shoulder-length hair was tied in a high ponytail. She had accessorized with a bead necklace and pink earrings.

Meera, on the other hand, was a tomboy who loved mystery novels, played basketball and dreamt of becoming a detective when she grew up. She kept her wavy hair short. She wore a pair of dark blue jeans and a pale green top for the journey.

Meera thought Tara was really boring at times and Tara thought Meera was bossy most of the times, but they loved each other to the bits and were best friends.

*

They were travelling alone for the first time. They had wanted to spend their summer vacation at Dharamshala, with Uncle Jeet Singh, Aunt Vimmy, and cousins Samir and Deepa, but their parents could not take a break from work.

After a lot of discussion and drama by the girls, their parents had agreed to send them on their own.

They boarded a deluxe bus at 5AM from New Delhi. The driver and conductor had assured their parents that they would keep an eye on the girls and make sure they got down at the right stop once they reached their destination. The girls slept through half the journey but after they crossed the Punjab border, the view outside changed dramatically.

The dusty roads changed into light grey; and the dull green trees slowly turned into brighter shades of green. Tara was mesmerized by the change and wouldn't move her head back to straight position.

Meanwhile, Meera thought it was a good opportunity to catch up on some reading. But after a while she realized the open book of Nature outside would put any bestseller to shame.

When the bus driver stopped at Kangra for a quick cup of tea, the girls grew restless. After all, Dharamshala was only fifteen kms away and when one is approaching the desired destination, one wants to move faster instead of going slower.

Tara threw an irritated glance at the driver who was slowly walking towards a small roadside tea-stall.

Meera decided to get down, to stretch her legs. She walked a few steps and found that she was standing near a make-shift cobbler shack. She looked around idly, when something odd caught her eye. Between the old, beaten up shoes was a new, expensive looking pair of shoes. It was fluorescent green in colour, with a huge golden buckle in the shape of the letter 'G'.

Meera stared and thought, 'Unusual! This must be a real fashion statement in this area!' She was still smiling to herself when she saw the man who had come to pick up the shoes. He was an ordinary looking local who certainly wasn't the one who could have dared to make the 'fashion statement'. To pay for the mending fee, he took out a single, pink, thousand rupee note from his battered wallet.

Meera could not believe her eyes. 'Something is really out of place here,' thought Meera.

The cobbler gave the man a sarcastic smile and said, "Do you think I have change for that amount? I want ten rupees in change. And get it from somewhere yourself."

Meera wanted to see what the man would do next but her attention was diverted by the sharp honk of the bus, which meant they were ready to leave.

She quickly ran towards the bus and saw that her sister was already at the door, probably looking for her.

Tara gave Meera a mean look which meant she didn't approve of her getting out in the first place and that she would certainly use it somewhere to her own advantage!

After a really slow and curvy ride of forty-five minutes, they finally heard the bus conductor shout, "Next stop, Kachahri Adda!" He then gestured to the girls to remind them that it was their stop too.

Tara checked the note their mother had written for them. They had to get down at Kachahri Adda, which was in Lower Dharamshala, where their cousin would come pick them up and take them home. Meanwhile, Meera had kept her novel and water bottle in her bag and was placing their suitcase near the door of the bus.

As she did so, she saw a bag under the first seat near the door. There was something familiar about it. It was exactly the same fluorescent green colour as the colour of the shoes she had seen at the cobbler's!

'Well, what are the odds?' she wondered. She stared at it and saw that it also had a huge golden 'G' buckle at the front, just like the shoes. She looked up to see who could possibly be its owner, but a sudden jolt imbalanced her and she was about to fall, when Tara helped her to her feet.

*

The bus had stopped at their destination. The girls hurriedly stepped down and the conductor helped them with their bags. They thanked him and then started looking around for their cousin, Samir.

Tara spotted Samir a few feet away, but he had already seen them and was running towards them with a huge grin on his face. The girls were very fond of Samir, and his younger sister, Deepa.

Samir was thirteen years old and adored his smart 'city' cousins. He also shared Meera's interest for mystery novels, and apart from being on the cricket team, was the captain of the trekking club at school. He was tall, athletic, and had closely-cropped hair.

Samir had been eagerly awaiting their arrival so that the three of them could have a great vacation. On their arrival, they exchanged quick hellos and then started walking away from the noisy bus-stop towards his home.

Samir's home in Sham Nagar was a twenty minute walk from the bus-stop at Kachahri Adda. He picked up their suitcase and Meera and Tara carried one handbag each. Although taxis were available at the bus stop, they preferred to walk, as the route was scenic.

The road was steep, so they had to be careful with the luggage. They walked very slowly, taking in the beauty of Dhauladhar range and chatting happily about school and friends. Their long journey had tired them but the anticipation of a wonderful vacation overpowered the fatigue. When they reached home, they were greeted by their aunt, uncle and a very excited Deepa. They freshened up quickly and their aunt served hot *samosas* and ginger tea.

After an early dinner and long chats, everyone went to bed. Meera and Tara shared the guest room. They were looking forward to the next morning as they went to sleep.

CHAPTER 2

The Buddha Statue

In that village near Kangra, two men visited the old monastery of Deevar. At a shabby little tea stall in the corner, they ordered tea and puffs. They kept sitting there.

The *chai wala* asked, seeing how their eyes were focused on the movement in and around the Buddhist temple, "Are you visiting the monastery or just passing through the village?"

"Oh, we are supposed to meet some friends here. They seem to be running late," they said, their look not encouraging the *chai wala* to ask any more questions. They left as the sun started to go down, making an excuse that apparently their friends were very late.

The tea stall owner closed shop by 7PM and the only source of light outside the monastery went out.

It was now pitch-dark near the old monastery. It was one of the early monasteries that were set up in the area. The monastery was small, and now in shambles. The monks had also relocated to other, bigger monasteries, where there was better accommodation, and shifted the ancient books and scriptures along with them.

Only one old monk lived in the small one-room monastery to keep the essence of the place alive. That monk had been in that monastery ever since he was very young, so when he was also asked to leave the monastery to move with the others, he refused. He wanted to keep the monastery operational till he could manage. With the limited means, it was getting difficult to do so with every passing day. But he was carrying on.

The small room was home to an ancient idol, a few scriptures and framed pictures of Lord Buddha. Although the significance of the place lay in its ancient roots, yet it was in an ignored state now.

No one could suspect any threat to the holy place or the holy man who guarded it.

*

The two men waited till they were sure that there was no one around. They entered the small gate of the monastery. It was only 7.30 in the evening, but night falls suddenly on the mountains and it becomes very dark almost immediately.

The old monk was in the small room, chanting from the scriptures, which he had placed under the dim light of a table lamp. The yellow light of a bulb hanging overhead changed its intensity according to the fluctuation in the input of electricity.

The monk chanted his prayers while the two men waited outside the door without moving. After a while, he got up and went inside his room-cum-kitchen, to cook his dinner. The men had to wait some more time before he finished his dinner and finally switched off the lights in the prayer room. He kept on talking to himself the whole time and only when his voice became quiet inside his room did the men enter the prayer room.

One of them twisted a small torch he was carrying, to throw light in the prayer room. He moved slowly on his toes, careful to avoid making any noise, or banging against anything on the floor. The prayer mats on the floor absorbed the sound of the footsteps. The other one kept looking towards the monk's room to ensure he would not notice the beam of light in the main room. The monk was already deep in sleep and his soft snores were audible, thus assuring them that they wouldn't be discovered.

The second man now switched his torch on as well. He moved it around till it rested on a small Buddha statue placed respectfully on a pedestal. Even in the dim light of the torch, it glittered in its full glory. The man stepped back and aimed the beam on the floor to make way for the first man, so that he could make a grab at the statue.

This man quietly tip-toed to the platform and picked up the statue from its base. He was carrying a muslin cloth and a cotton bag in his backpack and he quickly wrapped the statue, first in the muslin cloth, and then placed it inside the cotton bag. He then placed the padded statue in his backpack and nodded to his companion that they should be moving now.

The two moved out of the prayer room, switched off their torches and looked around. It was dark, and so quiet that they could hear the faint snores of the monk coming from inside. They stood there for a couple of seconds till their pupils got adjusted to the dark, and then slowly and surely moved towards the main gate. They jumped over the small gate and started walking fast, into the darkness.

Within a few minutes, they reached a street where an old jeep was parked. They jumped inside the jeep, started it and were on the State Highway in no time.

On the backseat of the jeep rested a 500 year old Buddha statue, wrapped in cloth, and tucked inside a backpack.

CHAPTER 3

Backpack in the Forest

Tara was dreaming about a trekking trip on the Dhauladhars. The air was cool and clear and it was very quiet, except for the continuous chirping of birds. Then, she heard Deepa calling out to her. 'Why did we bring Deepa to this difficult trek?' Tara was confused!

But then she realized that she was being shaken by Deepa, "Get up *Didi*, come on, don't waste time." Tara woke up to find Deepa almost sitting on top of her, excited, and laughing at her confusion.

Meera was already up and was sitting in the verandah staring at the orange-gold sky, waiting for it to change colours. She was trying to capture this beauty forever and make it a part of her memory.

Although the girls hated getting up early in the morning at their home in New Delhi and used to sleep till 8.30AM on Sundays; they loved to get up early in Dharamshala to enjoy the mornings in their complete glory.

This verandah was very special for the girls. It had a great view of the snow-capped mountains and the tiny flowing streams. They could hear morning bells and the sounds of *aarti* from a temple atop a hill.

Tara and Deepa joined Meera in the verandah. Their aunt and uncle also came there with their tea and newspapers. Samir was still sleeping. Meera picked up the local newspaper to see what events were scheduled during their stay.

According to the newspaper, an exhibition and a puppet show were being held in Dharamshala, during the coming week.

Meera shrugged and dismissed both the events in her mind. She was contemplating more adventurous ideas when her eye caught a tiny piece of news, 'Tourist Home's room ransacked, guest missing . . . ! Tourist Home, a budget guest house in Upper Dharamshala has come into the limelight because a French tourist has gone missing. No one noticed anything amiss till the housekeeping boy found the room turned upside down last Sunday as if someone had been desperately searching for something there. After he informed the manager, they checked the guest register and other employees to realize that the guest in Room No. 136 had not been seen in the guest house for the last three days. His absence was not noticed because many tourists checked in for ten-fifteen days, left their luggage there, and went out for days, for trekking, adventure sports, etc. But his room was vandalized so it is clear that something shady is going on. Police have registered a case and are looking for the tourist.'

Meera was a little unhappy after reading this news because Dharamshala was a peaceful little hill station and coming here was always associated with relaxation. Any mishap would tarnish its impeccable reputation, which was an unbearable thought.

"What are you reading?" asked Uncle Jeet. Jeet Singh was a senior officer in the Secret Service. He was born and brought up in Dharamshala and was well versed with its streets and people. He was also a well-known and highly respected person among the local residents.

"I am reading about this French tourist case." Meera replied.

"Yes, we have a few clues. After all, it is difficult to keep track of tourists' activities with the everyday increase in their numbers," he said.

Meera wanted to discuss this some more when Aunt Vimmy, interrupted, "So what do you want for breakfast?"

"I want *aalo parantha,*" chirped Tara, followed by clapping from Deepa, indicating her approval.

"OK! And what are your plans for the day?" Aunt Vimmy asked.

"We should go to McLeod Ganj today, what say?" Tara asked Meera, and Meera nodded lazily, as if compromising her choice.

She had been unable to finish her conversation with Uncle Jeet because he had received a phone call from one of his friends in the police. She had heard him say, “Yes, I know! There are many temples that have been targeted in the last few months. The thieves are good at their ground work because all the targeted temples have no security but have centuries old idols housed there, unguarded at night.

“I’m familiar with the monastery that you are telling me about, it was almost shut down after the big earthquake of ’82 because of the damage to it. It was kept open due to the sentiments attached to it and, in fact, recently there had been talks of closing it down for sure, because it is in shambles. Maybe, just maybe, the thieves also knew that the idol would be moved soon to a more secure temple or monastery.”

He seemed to be discussing a theft that Meera had not seen reported in the newspaper. “Yes, if you don’t find the idols within this week, you can assume they’ve hidden it somewhere till this matter quiets down. Anyway, they have changed their modus operandi since the last string of thefts. This time, they have not drugged the monk to make sure he can’t identify them later. All the best, Virender, let’s meet sometime soon, it’s been a long time.” Disconnecting the phone, Uncle Jeet had joined them at the dining table.

After a typical breakfast of *aaloo parantha, aam ka achar*, *dahi* and *meethi sewanyian*, the girls, Samir and Deepa were ready to leave. They were already torturing Samir for getting up late and delaying them by almost an hour.

Samir protested, "Oh come on, I'll make it up to you . . . how about taking a taxi instead of a bus to save time? OK, OK. I'll pay the taxi fare, now leave me alone."

Tara had already started laughing, "We are just pulling your leg. Don't be silly, the taxi fare will be split three ways."

Deepa asked, "How much money will I have to pay, *Didi*?" She seemed worried, and was trying to calculate the money she had in the piggy bank.

"Sweetie, you don't have to pay anything, just enjoy yourself . . . that would be your share." Tara said, bringing the smile back on Deepa's face.

*

They hired a taxi for McLeod Ganj in Upper Dharamshala, which appeared on the tourist map after His Holiness the Dalai Lama established his government-in-exile there.

Apart from the Dalai Lama's monastery and temple, there was a huge bazaar famous for Tibetan handicrafts and *momos, thukpa* and other Tibetan delicacies, Tibetan medicines and turquoise silver jewellery. A little further from the bazaar was

Bhagsu Nag, an ancient temple and a big waterfall. Also, the drive itself was so beautiful that one could spot tourists getting down to take pictures by the *deodar* forests and the rivulets.

After a round-and-round drive to the top, they got down at McLeo market. They decided to stroll down, as Tara wanted to buy a silver trinket for herself and a souvenir for home.

She was looking around in a small shop, trying on a pair of old silver earrings with turquoise and coral stones, when a huge man brushed past her and headed straight towards the displayed necklaces. He tried a few, looking at himself critically again and again.

Tara lost interest in her earrings and began secretly looking at this man engrossed in self-beautification. He was approximately six feet tall, sturdily built, with golden-brown hair, and was wearing shorts and a t-shirt.

All of a sudden, he turned to Tara, and asked, "Hi, can you help me decide which one looks best on me?"

Tara was a little taken aback, she had never spoken to a foreigner before and it was difficult to understand his accent but she nodded a yes, and looked at what he was wearing. He had four necklaces on, all of which were long and heavy.

Tara had a weakness for turquoise so she instinctively pointed towards the one with crude chunks of blue turquoise woven in a thick silver chain. In the centre was a huge chunk of coral. The man happily finalized and bought that necklace, thanked Tara and went off.

Tara was all the more surprised at how casual and easy it was for him to buy something that an unknown teen had picked out. 'Wow,' she thought, and quickly paid for her earrings. She joined the others and told them her story, spicing it up by making her conversation with the foreigner longer than it actually was. They were all a little surprised and Deepa stared at her, highly impressed.

They proceeded towards the Dalai Lama's monastery and temple. The monastery had a huge prayer hall where Buddhist monks read holy books, chanted and prayed. It created serenity and peace in the monastery for all. There was also a huge golden statue of Lord Buddha which embodied beauty and piousness in one. All four of them were in silent awe the entire time they were inside. Then they decided to quietly sit down in the prayer hall before leaving.

Meera got into a meditative mood once she sat in a corner. She got a clear view of Lord Buddha from her spot. She started thinking about this little world in McLeod Ganj, so different and yet so much a part of the surroundings. She was lost in her own thoughts when her instincts told her someone was watching her.

She turned to see a young monk, not more than seven-eight years old, with his head shaven, and in a yellow shirt with maroon robe, smiling at her. She smiled back at him. He turned back, bowed before Lord Buddha and started praying. Meera too bowed and signalled to her cousins and sister to come out.

It was lunch time and the calories from the breakfast seemed to have vanished. They decided to have lunch in one of the most famous noodle cafés nearby. It was a roof-top restaurant, very famous for its noodles and soup. They chose a corner table overlooking a forest of *deodars*. It looked like a green painting, calm and serene to the eyes.

Samir suddenly said "*Arre,* guys, how about a picnic trek to Bhagsu Nag? We can pack a good lunch, water, and coffee and enjoy ourselves near the waterfall. The trek to the waterfall is also interesting. It would be a real adventure."

Bhagsu Nag was a temple and a waterfall, a few kms away from McLeod Ganj. The trip from the road took a long time to reach but there was also a short-cut that was steep and adventurous and the locals used it. Youngsters looking for some outing could also be seen exploring the area.

*

Meera was listening to Samir who was talking about a trek to Bhagsu Nag when she spotted something out of place in the forest view. It was a speck of moving maroon, or was it yellow? She stared harder . . .

"Hey, finish your soup, Meera." Tara reminded her.

"Look guys, there is someone very deep in the forest," she replied.

Everyone now focused on the forest. Deepa took out her newly purchased toy binoculars and put them to good use. She could not see very clearly but she kept adjusting it till she could make out a vague figure. "*Didi*, I think it is a little monk," she exclaimed excitedly.

"Let me see," Samir took her binoculars. He looked through them and said, "Yes, it is indeed a young Lama, probably going for a walk in the forest. No big deal!"

It was in fact no big deal because these monks knew the area like no one else. Still, all four kept their eyes on the forest.

Meera could not take her eyes off the Lama. After ten minutes Meera gasped. She stared hard, yes, she was right! There he was . . . the same young Lama who had caught her attention in the monastery. He was now within view, walking slowly, the same, calm smile on his face.

"Guys, I think I saw this Lama in the monastery," she said quietly, still unsure of what she was saying.

"Not possible, *Didi*, even if he got out at the same time as we did, how could he have reached deep inside the forest, so fast? He must be a different Lama, you are mistaken. After all, they all look alike with the same robes and bald heads. You can't possibly remember a face so distinctly that you saw so briefly."

"Yes, maybe, or maybe he knows a shortcut," Meera also rationalized.

"Let's get moving now," Tara said. She was looking forward to a picturesque walk to Forsyth Ganj, just below McLeod Ganj. It was home to an old church and they wanted to visit it before heading home. After paying their bill, they started walking, slowly taking in the view as they did so.

Deepa skipped for the most part of the walk back to the 'St. John in the Wilderness Church'. Built amidst tall and very old *deodars,* it was a beautiful, old structure, with painted, coloured window panes. There was still a small graveyard at one side of the church.

The gang took a break from the walk and Deepa and Meera went inside to sit down for a few minutes. Tara and Samir decided to look around.

*

As they walked, Samir noticed something out of place in the trees. It looked like a bright blue balloon stuck in the branches. He instinctively walked towards the tree. On getting closer, he realized it was a blue backpack.

He lifted it out from the branches, and looked around, but there wasn't anyone to claim the bag.

"Hello, is anyone here? Whose backpack is this?" He called out into the emptiness, but there was no answer.

"What are you doing?" someone called out from behind.

"Ooo . . . aa . . . h . . . !" Samir jumped in surprise and turned around to see Tara.

"What are YOU doing? You scared me!" he said.

This really amused Tara. "Just scaring you, that's all," she said, and smiled. Samir smiled back with relief. Both of them waited for someone to return for the bag but no one did. After a few minutes they returned with the backpack to the church, to join Meera and Deepa.

Meera was already anxious at their delay. Samir narrated what had happened and they decided to give the bag to the police.

"How about taking a peep inside?" Samir's curiosity was getting the better of his judgement.

"I don't think we should, you had no business picking it up and bringing it with you in the first place, Samir," Meera said sternly.

"Oh come on . . . maybe we can find out the name of the owner," urged Tara.

Meera gave in and Samir quickly unzipped the bag. There were some clothes, a shaving kit and a few notes on Dharamshala . . . a typical tourist bag, no sign of any identification, no wallet, nothing to trace its owner. "Well, it is of no use," shrugged Meera.

Samir said, his hand still inside the bag, "Oh, I think some talcum powder has spilled inside." He pulled out his hand and saw some white powder on his fingertips.

"Whatever! Now let's give it to the police and go home. It is getting late," Meera concluded.

They hurried to the nearest police station. They handed over the bag to the constable present, narrated their account, left their address and boarded a local bus to Kachahri Adda.

*

"It was a very good day, *Di*," chirped Deepa.

"Yes, it was good fun," Tara smiled.

It was almost 6.30PM and the sun was setting, looking like an orange ball behind the mountains and giving an orange glow to the snow.

Meera was staring hard at the orange reflection when suddenly a thought hit her. "Sam, we found talcum powder in the bag, but there was no container, was there?"

"No *Di*, there wasn't. Maybe it just fell out, after all, the bag was hanging from the tree for who knows how long," Samir added thoughtfully.

Tara and Deepa began to run, to see who would reach home first. Meera still couldn't shake the idea of talcum powder but no container, but Samir had started to hum a tune, so she kept her thoughts to herself.

When they reached home, their aunt was anxiously waiting for them at the door. "Are you alright? Inspector Kumar from the police station at Forsyth Ganj had called. He wants to meet you all tomorrow."

"Yes, Mumma, we had an adventure . . . ee . . ."Deepa shouted, and Samir quickly explained to his mother what had happened.

"Well, you have to meet him tomorrow. Inspector Kumar suspects that the powder might be cocaine. It is very serious business."

They were shocked and Meera involuntarily whispered, "I knew it!" Samir and Tara were equally shocked. Deepa didn't understand why everyone had turned grim. She took her chocolate milk to the living room and started watching cartoons.

After refreshingly hot tea and choco-chip cookies, Meera, Tara and Samir sat down to ponder over the events of the day.

"We'll have to wait until tomorrow to understand what is going on," Meera said.

They had a quiet dinner and went to bed quickly after that. They were very tired and the anticipation of the next day was making all of them anxious. Within minutes they were fast asleep.

CHAPTER 4

The little Lama

The morning was a busy one for everyone. Uncle Jeet was taking the kids to meet Inspector Kumar at the police station. He had decided to leave Deepa at home with Aunt Vimmy, who was a little worried about the unexpected involvement of the children in such a case. But Uncle Jeet assured her that this was a routine and necessary interview.

The three teens hopped into the car, a little nervous, yet excited. They were quiet all through the ride to Forsyth Ganj, trying to think how to narrate their stories. At the police station, they found Inspector Kumar waiting for them. He turned out to be an acquaintance of Uncle Jeet. They exchanged a few pleasantries and got down to business. Since Samir and Tara had discovered the bag, they explained how they had seen it hanging from a tree branch at the church and retrieved it. Then Meera told him why they had opened the bag and about the contents of the bag.

"I must say, Sir, that it was very strange that we found the bag there," Samir said.

"Why do you say that?" Inspector Kumar asked.

"For one, it was sort of inside the forest, though not very deep inside, but no one goes that far from the church. Tourists stick to the church, the graveyard area and the clearing around it, but no one ventures inside the forest," Samir said. "And I don't think any of the locals go that side too, there was no sign of a used pathway in that direction. Why would anyone slow their pace by going there?"

"Maybe it is a lesser known short-cut," Tara added.

"No, *Di*, if it were a shortcut, there would be some signs. If anyone had to go that side, they would have to cut bushes and thorns. That would be impractical." Samir was sure about his theory.

Inspector Kumar was listening thoughtfully, and said, "I also think that it is not a short cut. Besides, there is no explanation why the bag was abandoned there. It has been almost twenty-four hours since you found it, and no one has come to the police station to claim it. There is no I.D. inside. Just some white powder and four hundred US dollars."

"What is this about the powder being cocaine, Inspector Kumar? Is it confirmed yet?" Uncle Jeet asked.

"No, it has been sent to the lab. It will take some time to find out what it is exactly. But my experience says it is cocaine," Inspector Kumar sounded sure. "I don't know what is going on around here, really. Did you hear about the missing French tourist? And now this, turning into a drug case . . . I'm sure you have some clue about this, Mr. Singh!" Inspector Kumar probed Uncle Jeet to get some inside information.

Uncle Jeet dodged the question, "We have some information but nothing that I can disclose at the moment."

After all the questions were answered, Inspector Kumar wanted them to show the exact spot and the tree where the bag was found. They hopped into the police van and reached the church within minutes.

Samir and Tara led the way while Inspector Kumar along with two constables and Uncle Jeet followed them.

*

Meera walked slowly behind this party. She could feel the tension in the air as opposed to the excitement of the previous day.

Her eyes caught something appearing and disappearing amongst the trees ahead of her. She slowed her pace to catch a better glimpse, it seemed as though a blob of maroon was moving.

'Was it the little Lama again?'

She felt a strange sense of fear as she tried to follow the moving figure. It went inside a group of trees. She kept following it, moving as fast as she could.

After a brisk walk of about five minutes, the moving figure stopped and looked back at her. It was still too far from her to make out if it was the same Lama, but it was certainly a young Lama.

She started running towards him, hoping to catch up with him, now that he had stopped moving.

He went behind a tree as if to tease her. She was where he had been, but now she couldn't see the Lama anywhere. She looked around hard, behind trees and big rocks, but it was as if he had disappeared.

'What is going on here? This is weird,' she thought.

She looked around for a few moments. There was no sign of anyone, and she had not only drifted away from her group but also lost track of the person who she was following for no apparent reason. She was alone in the middle of the forest.

'Great!! I am definitely in trouble!' she thought, and as she started tracing back her steps, she spotted something black on the ground. She picked it up and found that it was a rexine travel pouch. She opened it to find some documents and some foreign currency and . . . a passport!

She heard someone calling her name, "Meera, where are you? Meera! Meeeerrra!"

"Please come here . . ."she shouted back.

After a couple of minutes she heard footsteps approaching her.

"I'm here, look what I found," she shouted again.

The group joined her, but no one shared her enthusiasm.

"Meera, you know better than this! Going into the forest on your own can be dangerous!" Her uncle was clearly very angry.

Tara too gave her a mean look.

"I'm sorry, Uncle Jeet, but I was following a young Lama. He ran away but look what I found! Travel documents, a passport, and some currency!" She had everything lying open in front of her.

Inspector Kumar took the bag and opened the passport. He went strangely silent for a few seconds and then started placing orders, "Seal this area; mark the spot where we found this pouch and comb the area with more men and get two sniffer dogs . . ."

"What is the matter?" Uncle Jeet demanded.

"The passport belongs to the missing French tourist," Inspector Kumar said in a low voice.

CHAPTER 5

An Evening at the War Memorial

The ride back home was grimmer than the one to the police station. Uncle Jeet looked very worried. After the passport of the French tourist was found, the chances of the tourist being in grave danger were very high.

It also meant that something foul was at play in Uncle Jeet's hometown. He was eager to drop the three of them home and rush to his office to gather more information on the matter.

The children too were eager to reach home and discuss the events of the day and their connection to the bag found in the forest.

Meera was struggling with her own thoughts of the young Lama. 'Was it my imagination? No, I definitely saw him. I wasn't imagining it. He looked back at me as if to check where I was and I think he led me to the passport.'

It was past lunch time and they were feeling hungry when they reached home. Uncle Jeet didn't come home for lunch and rushed to his office.

Aunt Vimmy greeted them at the door, "Here you are. We've been waiting for you. I've cooked *rajmah chawal*. So, how did everything go?"

"It was all fine. But you know, Mummy, what Meera *Didi* found!" Samir narrated the day's events to her quickly.

Their aunt looked worried, and said, "That is all OK, but no wandering alone anywhere, girls. It doesn't sound safe."

"Yes, Aunty," Meera replied.

Tara was already thinking ahead about their evening plans. "How about we all go to *Shaheed Smarak*, the War Memorial, around 5PM?" she asked.

"Sounds good, but first *rajmah chawal* it is!" Meera had washed up and was already serving Deepa and herself. Sam, Tara and Aunt Vimmy joined them and the hungry adventurers devoured the delicious lunch.

After they'd had food to their hearts' content, they went for a nap and all was quiet in the house for about an hour. Tara was the first to wake up at around 4.30PM and she started to wake everyone else too. All four of them were back in a mood for fun by the time they left home to go to War Memorial at around 5PM.

It took them about half-an-hour to reach there. They didn't realize they had been walking for so long because they were busy talking about school and friends. Deepa didn't complain of being tired.

*

They bought tickets to go inside. The War Memorial was built in the honour and memory of martyrs and war heroes. It was a peaceful place, with a huge rock sculpture in the middle of a water body, highlighted by multi-coloured spotlights. On one side of the sculpture there was a pine forest, and a flower-laden hill on the other.

"Look, guys, it's beautiful. Let's sit here," Tara said, almost in a whisper. Everyone looked in that direction. The setting sun and rows and rows of roses on the hill created a serene and calming effect. They sat down on a nearby bench from where they could see the view clearly. People had started to come for their evening walks now; there were tourists and locals both who never got tired of this place.

After a few minutes on the bench, Meera told the others of her encounter with the young Lama earlier in the day. "I know it sounds very mysterious and illogical but I know what I saw. There was definitely someone who led me to the passport. I don't know if it was the same Lama from McLeod Ganj or it was someone else but I really believe I was taken there purposely by a mysterious person."

Tara and Samir didn't know what to say, and Deepa was a little scared. "Do you think he was a ghost, *Didi*?" she asked.

"No, Deepa, I'm sure he wasn't a ghost. There is no such thing as ghosts. He didn't do any harm; he just wanted me to find that passport. Maybe he is a fast runner or very shy to talk to us. But he was trying to help. Don't be scared," Meera assured Deepa.

"What do you think is the link between the missing French tourist, the bag, the drugs in the bag and that forest?" Samir looked at Meera and Tara for an answer.

"I think the French tourist was a drug addict who was carrying drugs in his bag. He took too much and went crazy or felt unwell, so he was trying to find his way out but under the influence, he went deeper into the forest," Tara said.

"Still doesn't explain why his hotel room was upside down, his bag was found in one part of the forest, and his passport pouch in another." Meera argued.

"Maybe someone was after him. They might have tried to search for drugs in his hotel room, then found him in the forest and snatched his bag. But there was nothing inside, so they took his papers. He probably ran off into the forest to save his life. They might have gone after him and dropped his papers on the way." Samir seemed to have the answers to all the questions.

But Meera had something else to question, "How did they get the drugs in the first place? And who are these 'they' you are referring to? I don't know Sam, everything sounds so fishy!"

"That it is, *Di*," he replied.

They sat around thinking and then walked towards the small café near the exit, Meera treated everyone to ice cream shakes and they left the War Memorial to go home.

CHAPTER 6

The Treasure Hunt

The kids were excited. Sam's friend, Anurag, had invited them all for his birthday party. His residence was in the cantonment area near McLeod Ganj. It was an old spacious mansion and Sam and Deepa just loved spending time there. Once they reached there, Meera and Tara understood why; there was so much to explore around the house. The house was a haven for the kids, with a frequently updated library and games for them.

The architecture was British and the mansion stood proudly amidst the *deodar* forest. On one side was a badminton court, and a small pathway connected the house to a series of lanes leading to the main road. The house was not visible from the main road.

Samir had borrowed his mother's cell phone for the day. He did not have a cell phone of his own, but whenever he went out for the entire day, his mother would give him her cell phone. To make the best of such opportunities, he had downloaded a few popular games too.

After the big birthday bash, Anurag had arranged a game of Treasure Hunt. He had scattered clues all around the house which led to the map of a hidden treasure somewhere in the forest which would eventually lead to, of course, a treasure!

The invitees were divided into four groups and the party was thoroughly enjoying this Treasure Hunt. The clues were interesting and well hidden, and with every clue the excitement increased.

*

Tara and Sam led the race and were already in the forest, searching for the object that had to be found on the basis of:

'Under the blue; beside the blue;
Under the green; beside the green;
Under the red; beside holy reds;
I sit and wait; I sit and wait for you.'

Sam scratched his head to figure out what to make of the riddle. Tara, however, was busy studying the 'blue' 'green' and 'red'. She looked hard into the spread of the *deodar* forest, a vast spread of green and caught a glimpse of the blue sky beyond.

She smiled and asked Sam, "Do you know if a stream flows through the forest Sam?"

"Actually it does. What are you thinking?" Sam looked at her expectantly.

"Let's find the stream first," Tara coaxed Sam.

They ventured deep into the forest, following Sam's instincts and limited knowledge of the forest. Fifteen minutes later, they could hear the soothing sound of flowing water and they hurried towards it.

"Now tell me what does the clue lead to?" Sam inquired

"It's under the blue . . . that is blue sky, and beside the blue stream; under the green tree, near a green house or landmark of some sort. I have a feeling we will find a temple or a holy mark close by, which would explain the 'holy reds'," Tara smiled.

"Wow! That was a wild deduction. But there is, in fact, an ancient, dilapidated monastery upstream. I think you've solved the riddle, *Di*. Let's move fast, I'm so excited!" Sam started sprinting northwards, where he remembered the monastery to be.

Tara ran after him, ignoring the tiny weeds sticking to her corduroy trousers. 'These weeds will have to be pulled out once I reach home, or they will definitely ruin my beautiful trousers', she made a mental note of this fact even as she ran.

"Hurry up, *Di*, I can hear voices. I don't want to lose this race," Sam screamed, as he saw the damaged, dull-green roof of the ancient monastery just twenty-five metres from his sight.

As Tara joined him, he whispered, "Under the green monastery, beside the green tree," and directed her attention to a huge tree that covered the monastery like a huge umbrella.

Tara had never seen that monastery before. It looked ancient and deserted, with its damaged green roof which seemed to be at the verge of coming down, it was in such shambles. Mould and fungi covered the walls, and from a distance, the entire structure appeared to be a shade of green. There appeared to be two heavy doors with equally ancient heavy locks protecting whatever was inside.

Despite the neglect, Tara felt that there was something very spiritual about the place. Tara and Sam circled the perimeter of the monastery and found the main entrance door. This side was lined with tiny Buddha statues and some flower pots.

'They must have been a pretty sight once,' thought Tara, but like the rest of the structure, only the remains of little red statues and the broken red flowerpots stood there as a witness of better times.

"It must be here," Sam pointed to a half-broken, dull-red flowerpot placed between two Buddha statues.

‘Under the red, beside holy reds,’ he muttered, and picked up the remains of the pot. Underneath, there was a shiny key and a note, ‘the chest of chestnut awaits!’

Sam started laughing, “This is the final clue, and we got it. There is a chest in Anurag’s living room. I’m guessing it is made of chestnut wood. Let’s rush back to the mansion, *Didi*.”

“Yes let’s go, I can hear voices, maybe some other group is nearby. Let them keep guessing where the last clue from ‘under the red’ went,” she giggled, as they walked away from the green monastery.

Had they paid more attention, they would have noticed that the voices were coming from inside the deserted monastery, where three men in black hoodies were waiting for the kids to leave.

One of the men was wearing fluorescent green shoes with a ‘G’ insignia.

CHAPTER 7

Three Hooded Men

When they saw Tara and Sam move away, one of them said, "Keep that pistol inside, they have gone. Let's finish the job and leave. I don't want to draw any attention to ourselves."

The three men quickly entered the room attached to the main hall of the monastery. The main hall was empty except for a few broken pieces of furniture. The room attached to the hall also did not have anything except for an old broken bookshelf kept in a corner.

They seemed to know what they were looking for. They moved the bookshelf and shone their torches on the wall behind it. The wall had a niche big enough for one person to fit in. The leader motioned to the smaller of the other two to get inside. The small man quickly got inside and disappeared for a few seconds while the two outside aimed their torch lights into the niche.

When he crawled back, he held in his hand a small statue of Lord Buddha. In the yellow lights of the torches, the old gold looked even more yellow. The turquoise and coral stones at the base glowed.

The three of them threw victorious glances at each other and quickly wrapped up the statue in a muslin cloth before placing it in the backpack of their leader.

They swiftly moved the bookshelf against the wall, turned off their torches and climbed out of the window in the main hall. The leader closed the window shut from outside and the three started walking quickly on a side-path in the forest.

*

Meanwhile, Meera, who had been teamed up with Eshaan, was running upstream towards the monastery.

"It has to be a place related to something holy according to the riddle. Are you sure there is a monastery in this direction?" Meera asked her partner.

"Yes, I'm sure it is close by."

"That's why Anurag sent Tara separately because she and I are the only ones not familiar with this forest. I'm sure all of you have explored this forest quite a few times," she chuckled.

"Yes, we often play warrior games here. It's a lot more fun than playing it on the XBox. Hey, look, there is that monastery."

Meera was very excited to see the monastery from a distance, when, from the corner of her eye, she noticed the three hooded men. They seemed to be moving fast in the opposite direction on a parallel path in the forest.

"Hello!" Meera called out instinctively. The men stopped in their tracks for a few seconds, surprised, and not sure how to react.

The leader responded, "Hi, what are you kids doing here?"

"We are playing Treasure Hunt, are you lost? Generally nobody takes this path," Eshaan asked loudly.

"No, no, we are fine. Thank you. You be safe now. Bye." The leader motioned to his two companions to keep walking.

"Bye," Eshaan waved.

The men moved away and carried on.

Meera also waved a goodbye to them and asked Eshaan, "Is this a shortcut to some place?"

"None that I am aware of," he replied.

She wanted to ask something further when Eshaan's cell phone rang. It was Sam. He asked for Meera, and when Meera took the cell from Eshaan he said, "*Didi,* where are you? Tara *Didi* and I found the final clue and we are back at Anurag's house. *We won!*" He was laughing on the other end of the phone.

"Oh!" Meera groaned, "Tara and Sam won. They've called back all teams to the house. Let's go back. Oh, we were so close!"

Both of them turned back and ran towards the house. All the guests at Anurag's birthday party were gathered in the living room when they reached his home. Anurag had called everyone after Tara and Sam returned with the final clue, opened the chestnut chest with the key and found their prize! They had won a big box of imported assorted chocolates and two Percy Jackson books.

Tara and Sam screamed and jumped with joy.

"Okay you both are gonna share it with us anyway!" Meera said with a smile.

Tara smirked, "OhhPhhlllease!!"

CHAPTER 8

The Man in Green Shoes

After a breakfast of French toast and Bournvita milk, the kids sat down to study and finish their vacation homework. Uncle Jeet had not yet left for office and seemed to be in a relaxed mood till the time his cell phone rang.

He picked up the phone and his expression became grim as soon as the conversation started. He went inside his study and shut the door.

Samir, Meera and Tara exchanged questioning glances and waited for him to reappear. He came out after about ten minutes and started getting ready and asked Aunt Vimmy to quickly give him a cup of tea. She asked him to wait so that she could serve French toast along with it, but he was already on another call and gestured a 'no' to her.

He said on the phone, "Good Morning, Sinha. I need you to take a team of four to the location I messaged earlier to you. Start a thorough search for any type of clues related to our case. I'll reach there in an hour. In particular, we must find the missing shoe and mark the location. It'll help us to track and trace the direction our man has come from. The shoe is very unusual in colour and should be easy to locate. Clear?"

No sooner had the words 'unusual shoe' left her Uncle Jeet's lips, Meera's eyes widened.

She almost sprang from her chair and said, "Is it a fluorescent green shoe, with a golden buckle?"

"What?" Uncle Jeet was angry and surprised at the same time.

Meera apologized, "I am sorry, to be eves-dropping, but I couldn't help overhearing you talking about an unusual shoe. I had seen a man with fluorescent green shoes near Kangra. If it is the same pair of shoes you are looking for, maybe I can help."

Uncle Jeet quickly showed her the picture that was sent to him on his cell earlier that morning. It was of a man lying on his belly. He seemed to be sleeping flat on the ground.

Meera could not make out his face, all she could see was that he was dressed in a simple t-shirt and jeans and that he had only one shoe on. The shoe was identical to the one that she had seen at the cobbler's near Kangra Bus stand.

"Yes, yes this is identical to the pair I saw the day we arrived in Dharamshala."

"You are coming with me, get ready in five minutes and, as we travel, tell me where in Kangra we need to go."

Before Samir and Tara could butt in and ask if they could accompany them, Uncle Jeet added, "And no, no one else is coming with me. I can't believe how involved you all are in this case and looks like it is just getting deeper."

Meera changed into her favourite dark blue pair of jeans and a purple top. She hurriedly slipped her feet into her blue sneakers and rushed out to join Uncle Jeet who was busy giving more instructions over the phone to someone at office, updating them about his changed plans.

He gestured to her to walk with him and waved a goodbye to Aunt Vimmy. Meera also waved a bye to everyone and ran after him, towards the official Scorpio parked outside, while he talked on the phone.

"Yes, I am taking my niece to Kangra, to the location where she saw the man with the shoes. I want you to message me a picture of our dead guy's face so that the cobbler can identify him."

The driver ran to open the door of the SUV and Meera and Uncle Jeet got inside. He asked Meera to narrate the exact account of what she had seen and heard that day.

Meera explained everything in detail—the villager with the shoes, how he gave one crisp, thousand rupee note to the cobbler, how the cobbler asked him to get change, and how the shoes and the note both seemed odd in that villager's hands.

She also remembered and added how she had bumped into a bag of the exact same colour and insignia on the bus while she was getting down at Kachahri Adda.

She said she could identify the villager and the cobbler but not the man on the bus because she hadn't seen his face.

Uncle Jeet listened carefully and as soon as his cell phone beeped with the message tone, he opened it to show Meera the close up shot of the dead man's face.

Meera was a bit hesitant but she looked carefully and couldn't recognize the face. "No, this is not that villager."

"OK, no problem! We'll have to investigate with that cobbler then."

*

They reached Kangra Bus stand in about half an hour and Meera directed the driver towards the cobbler's shack.

Uncle Jeet first showed the cobbler the photograph of the dead man on his cell phone and asked if he recognized him. The cobbler was taken aback to see a dead man's picture but said that he did not know him.

Then Uncle Jeet further asked if he remembered a villager who had come to collect green shoes, given earlier for mending. Meera added that he had given a thousand rupee note, and described the overall appearance of the man.

The cobbler immediately nodded his head, and said, "Yes, yes, *Sahib*, Ratan had brought a pair of green shoes a couple of days back. Shady little fellow that Ratan is! He is always involved in some kind of hanky-panky business."

"OK, can you give us his address?" Uncle Jeet asked impatiently.

The cobbler explained the way to Ratan's house and the driver noted the directions. Getting back into the SUV, Uncle Jeet immediately called his subordinate to inform him that they probably had identified a link in this case and went on to give further instructions.

Uncle Jeet's driver was a resourceful fellow, as he had to be, since he was also part of the Secret Service team. He followed the cobbler's instruction to the T, and within fifteen minutes they were stepping down from the Scorpio, in front of a small, *kacha* house with a slated roof. They knocked on the door and Ratan, the villager whom Meera had seen a couple of days ago, opened the door.

*

Ratan was visibly scared to see an authoritative figure at his door and voluntarily gave all the information that he had. He almost broke down when he saw the picture of the dead man.

"This is my cousin, Chandu, *Sahib*!" Ratan said, his voice breaking with emotion. "I do not know exactly what Chandu did for a living, but he was always involved with shady people."

"What about the green shoes? Where did he get them?" Uncle Jeet inquired.

Ratan said, his hands folded in front of him, "I know about the shoes, *Sahib*. Chandu had given them to me to be repaired and said some 'business link' had given them to him, along with a bag for safekeeping."

"Where is the bag?" Uncle Jeet asked, and Ratan immediately directed them to a small store room in one corner of the house.

Uncle Jeet's driver, who had accompanied them, went into the small store and brought out a medium-sized cloth bag, which appeared quite heavy for its size. The mouth of the bag was tied tight with a thick rope.

Uncle Jeet looked at Ratan, "You have not seen what was inside?"

"No, *Sahib*. I never look at Chandu's things. He is my cousin but also a shady fellow, so the less I know the better for me. I do not get involved in his business."

Uncle Jeet raised an eyebrow to show that he doubted the man's words. "Open it now," he ordered.

Ratan quietly complied. The colour drained from Ratan's face as he pulled out what the bag contained. Inside the bag, wrapped in many layers of cloth, was a very old brass idol of Lord Shiva. This is what he held out to them now.

The hunt for the man in green shoes had taken a nasty turn.

CHAPTER 9

Meera Connects the Dots

Meera quietly sat in the Scorpio listening to what Uncle Jeet was discussing with his colleagues on the phone during the drive back. They had come up with the theory that Chandu might have been involved with a gang of ancient idol thieves.

Reports of various such incidents were always coming from different parts of the State and although the police would get a break once in a while, they were not able to grab the whole gang.

Uncle Jeet had already sent the picture of the idol that was recovered from Chandu's bag, to his office for further distribution, aiming at positive identification.

"But Uncle Jeet, if Chandu was involved in this idol stealing racket then what was he doing in the McLeod Ganj forest? That means either there is a plan of another theft there or his buyers or bosses are in that area. After all, he has to be linked with that man in green bag somehow who was already in Dharamshala last week," Meera said, her young sleuth mind not at rest.

"Yes, I know. I have added that green bag man's name to the crime board already. We need more clues and fast. Even my officers and I feel there might be something cooking in that forest."

Uncle Jeet got down at his office and asked the driver to take Meera back home.

*

By the time she reached home, it was past lunch time and Aunt Vimmy was waiting for her to return so that they could have lunch together. Tara, Sam and Deepa were taking a nap after having had their lunch.

Her aunt asked her about what happened in Kangra and she told her about it in brief. As Meera finished her *aaloo gobhi* with *chapatti* and stuffed her mouth with some crunchy salad, her mind was racing. She came up with an idea and wanted to discuss that with the others but Aunt Vimmy told her to take a nap as well.

Meera lay in the bed thinking about the events of the last few days. Within a few minutes, she woke up startled, as something occurred to her.

She sneaked into Sam's bedroom and gently called out his name, "Sam! Sammy! Wake up . . ."

Sam woke up with a jerk and stared at her, "A-ohh! You scared me!"

"You scare easily . . ." she winked, and asked him to follow her out of the room without waking Tara and Deepa.

Once outside she closed the door behind them, and said, "Guess what I remembered?"

"Guess what I found out?" he asked a question in return.

"OK, you go first!" Meera said in a low, irritated tone.

Sam didn't seem to notice. "After you and Dad left, I started researching on the net about any possible drug peddling in and around Dhramashala.

"I found out that drug dealers had created a market for drugs in and around Manali many years ago and the prime target were tourists. Police became alert after many cases of tourists going missing came into the limelight in that area. The primary cause was that they got hooked on to these easily available cheap drugs and they would sometimes not return even after their visas expired. Since the police tightened the snooze around the neck of these drug peddlers, they wanted to shift base somewhere else.

"Meanwhile, McLeod Ganj has become a huge tourist attraction. Many tourists come here seeking *nirvana*. Unfortunately, quite a few also sought *nirvana* in the drug dens!"

Meera raised her eyebrows, this was indeed news.

Sam continued in a breathless hurry, as though he had a fund of information that he wanted to share immediately, "The drug peddlers have set up hidden shops in McLeod Ganj also.

"With that come not just illegal drugs, but also other vices in our beautiful town. Hence the bag that we discovered in the forest behind the church!" Sam concluded, in a very proud and satisfied tone.

"Hmm . . . all that research is pretty cool, I must say!" Meera tried to be sarcastic but she was impressed.

She spoke now, "Look, I told you I had just remembered something! The man in green shoes who was found dead in the forest this morning looked vaguely familiar to me, but I didn't pay attention to that instinct. I now realized why he looked familiar.

"The other day when we were playing Treasure Hunt, we crossed three men hurrying off into the forest. I felt it was odd since the path did not seem to be leading anywhere specific. I think that dead guy was among those three. And, if it is the same guy, there is definitely some idol stealing racket also active in these parts."

Sam was a bit contemplative, "You didn't notice his shoes when you saw him in the forest?"

"No, I was not paying attention. All I remember is that they were all in black hoodies. But do you realize one thing, he was found dead not very far from where I met him. That makes me sure that I am right on track."

Meera seemed determined, "Samir, I feel all of us have become part of this mystery whether we like it or not. Don't you think we should try to solve it or at least gather clues that'll help Uncle Jeet and Inspector Kumar? After all, we are familiar with the places of the crime and can do some digging up on our own."

"True that!! *Chalo,* I'm in, what do you suggest we do?" Samir asked, his eyes lighting up.

"Let's go back to McLeod Ganj tomorrow and do some snooping around in the church area where we found the bag, and then go to the area where I met Chandu. Maybe we'll find something interesting," Meera responded.

"Ok, done!" Sam said.

"What are you two talking about? Meera, when did you get back from Kangra?" Tara had walked in on them, having woken up from her nap.

Sam filled her in on the plan for the next day in a low voice, as Aunt Vimmy was also up and going into the kitchen to make evening tea for herself and milk-shakes for the kids.

Meera sneaked out into the verandah overlooking the Dhauladhars and sat down on the cemented edge. She loved that angle as it gave her the prefect view of the mountains minus the electric poles. The sun was setting behind the mountains and had coloured the snow orange.

It was all so calm and quiet and Meera felt a little saddened by the thought that hidden behind all the serenity and the simple beauty lay the ugliness of drugs. She also felt it was ironic that Himachal Pradesh, also known as *Dev Bhoomi*, was witnessing the stealing of the ancient idols of the Gods.

Meera projected a happy-go-lucky image but she was a deep thinker and sometimes would become lost in thoughts way beyond her years. She knew she couldn't do much when it came to this matter of stolen idols yet it was not in her nature to ignore the areas, where she thought she could make a difference.

'I'll find a way!' she mused.

The bell in the temple mountain made a loud '*tannnnn*' to announce the start of the *aarti.* She smiled 'Yes, I know, I'll find a way.'

"Why are you sitting there, pull a chair! Here's your milk-shake," said her aunt, handing her a large glass. She looked in the direction of the hill temple. "It is beautiful, isn't it?" she asked.

Meera nodded. Both sat in complete silence listening to the *aarti* which had started. It was not a record player blaring devotional songs based on popular Hindi movie songs but the traditional *aartis* sung in monotonous tones by the devotees.

Meera thought it was much better and kept trying to sing in her head, the few lines that she knew.

"Aunty, how is Dharamshala different from when you were in college?" she asked.

"Oh it's a world apart. There were fewer houses then, even fewer facilities. There were very few vehicles and hardly any pollution. We had to walk almost everywhere and it used to be tiring at times. Today, we have so much development but at the cost of a simpler lifestyle."

She paused and frowned, "And now, all this business with drugs and all . . . it is just awful . . ." She was echoing Meera's very thoughts.

"Mummmaaaa . . . ." Deepa screamed from inside, and her aunt got up and went inside, leaving Meera to think some more on her own.

She sat there till the sun had almost gone and the horizon was lined by a golden orange hue, in contrast to the darkening sky. Then she joined her sister and cousins in the living room to play Scrabble.

CHAPTER 10

Revisiting McLeod Ganj

Next morning Meera, Tara and Sam got ready quickly. They had already decided not to take Deepa along, as they had planned a long day ahead which involved a lot of walking through the forest.

Meera instructed Sam to fill up a bottle of water each for the three of them, and also take along a couple of note pads, pens, wet wipes, tissues, a hand sanitizer and chocolates. She had bought a Swiss Army knife a few months back and she kept it in her bag too. Tara looked at it and nodded her head sarcastically.

She told her aunt that since they had plans to walk up to the Bhagsu Nag waterfall, which was a narrow trek from McLeod Ganj, they wanted to leave Deepa at home. So, their aunt asked Deepa to help her with a trip to the vegetable market during the day instead of going the others. Deepa was visibly upset about it, but didn't throw a tantrum once Tara explained that they were planning to walk everywhere instead of taking a shared taxi.

The three of them left with Uncle Jeet who dropped them at the shared taxi stand.

Without wasting any time, they hopped in and were on their way to McLeod Ganj.

Once they reached there, Tara asked, "Why are we here? I mean, shouldn't we go to the church forest straightaway?"

Meera hesitated; she knew what she was about to say would sound silly, if not stupid.

"I was thinking if we could go back to the Dalai Lama's monastery and look for that young Lama. Maybe he could help us, if we find him."

"You are crazy, you know that?" Tara said loudly, "We don't know his name, how are we going to recognize him? And what are you going to do, go staring at all the Lamas there or ask all of them one by one if they have been playing hide and seek with us?"

"I know it's difficult, I am simply saying I want to try. The monastery is not far from here and the idea behind coming here is that we try and solve this thing. So we have to start somewhere," Meera said sheepishly.

She knew she was taking a shot in the dark with this Lama thing. She also knew that Tara and Sam expected her to come up with some sort of fool-proof plan but she was just relying on her gut feeling.

Sam looked at her and realized that she did not have a logical plan so he said, "It's OK, Tara

Di. What do we have to lose? It is not like it is an algebra problem. We will take it as it comes. If we get lucky, we'll find the Lama, if not we'll go to the forest and start our hunt there. No biggie!"

"No biggie, eh? Take her side even when you know it is just stupid," Tara gave him an evil look. "OK, fine. I guess we really don't have anything to lose. Let's go to the monastery," Tara rolled her eyes and Meera smiled.

*

They started walking towards the monastery and the colourful shops lined on both sides of that road caught Tara's attention. She walked slowly, looking at the open shacks on the road and admiring the beautiful colourful wares displayed.

"Why do you keep stopping? Do you have to buy anything? I don't understand this window-shopping habit, such a waste of time," Meera said in a hushed tone.

"You better not say anything to me. I am coming to the monastery with you because you want to go there!" Tara retaliated.

"Urrrgghhh!" Meera groaned, and walked away from Tara.

Sam had again borrowed his mother's cell phone and was busy texting a friend and giggling at some forwarded joke.

"I wish I had come alone, one is wasting time and the other is texting while walking," Meera groaned once again under her breath.

Meanwhile Tara had tried on a pair of danglers and was admiring herself in the mirror. She suddenly saw a familiar face in the mirror. She stopped looking at her reflection and stared at the reflection of the American she had spoken to, on the first day.

She felt very happy and quickly removed the danglers, kept them and the mirror back on the counter and started walking towards the American.

"What happened? You don't want these? I'll give you a good price, where are you going?" The shopkeeper called after her, but she kept walking towards the American.

"Hi," she said cheerfully.

The American turned to her.

He looked tired, unshaven, sleepy and confused. He obviously didn't recognize her so he just stood there, staring at her but he did not respond.

Tara felt a little embarrassed about running to talk to him but tried once again, "We had met the other day. I had helped you pick up a huge necklace."

"Ah, yes, yes, I'm sorry kiddo! I am a little tired. So how are you?" He smiled a weak smile.

"Oh I am good, we are just roaming around," Tara said. She had no idea what to talk to him about, so she asked, "So how long are you in India for?"

"For about another month now, hey, you know what . . . I lost that necklace you picked out for me that day, I guess you should help me today also."

*

By now Meera had realized that Tara was nowhere around them. She looked back and saw Tara talking to a stranger and called Sam, "Sammy, leave that stupid phone for a bit and see what Tara is up to."

Sam looked up and they started walking towards Tara. Tara was very happy to see them, primarily because she knew that they had not believed her the last time she said that the American had taken her help.

"Oh, this is my sister Meera, and my cousin Samir," she said as soon as they approached.

"Hello, my name is Greg," he said, and shook hands with both of them.

"And I still don't know your name," he smiled at Tara.

"Oh yes, I am Tara," Tara said with a chuckle.

'Okay enough with I am this, this is this, let's move!' Meera said in her head.

Meanwhile, Greg started asking questions about where they studied and Sam happily joined in. He had forgotten all about his phone and apparently about the monastery also.

"It's so nice to talk to you all. I was not feeling too well earlier but am feeling much better chatting with you all. How about us sitting down in that open café instead of standing here?"

Greg still didn't look too well to Meera, for he kept looking here and there and was scratching himself again and again.

Tara gave Meera a winning glace as if to say, 'See, I told you that this man spoke to me!'

But Meera was not ready to waste any more time and quickly took a decision, "Tara and Sam, why don't you guys carry on to the café with Greg while I go to the monastery alone and will join you once my work there is done."

Samir immediately objected "No, no . . . we'll all go together, I don't want you to go alone."

"You are going to the big monastery? I can also come with you," Greg said.

"I just want to go and sit there for a bit; I like the atmosphere in there. That's all. I thought since you were asking us all to join you at the café, maybe you wanted to chat, so I said that I'll carry on and catch up with you later," Meera said, in no mood to take Greg along.

Samir was confused as it was clear Meera wanted to go and Tara didn't.

Meera called Sam aside, "It would be better that you stay here with Tara, after all we don't know this Greg. She is just being stubborn and I don't want to get into an argument. I'll be back here soon," she said.

Sam just nodded his head. Meera waved to Tara and Greg, and started walking towards the monastery.

*

She kept on thinking about how she would search for the Lama, what she would have to do to find him. She reached there in less than ten minutes and after going through the security check and entering the complex, started looking around carefully.

The complex was huge and her quest was like trying to find a needle in a haystack. She started with the floor where she knew the Lamas chanted their prayers, and sat down in one corner. She had a clear view of all the young and older monks engrossed in their prayers and she started to look at them one by one.

She was scared that someone might ask her not to stare at them and to leave but she quietly sat and observed, nonetheless. The floor had a low seating arrangement with colourful, cotton-filled seating cushions on the floor lined up in front of the low tables where they could place the books. The hall had deep, warm colours on the walls and the floor, with stacks and stacks of ancient books displayed in the shelves mounted on the walls.

In the corners, brass oil lamps were placed. The multi-wick lamps were lotus shaped and the golden, flickering flames created a dramatic effect in the hall. The Lamas were meditating and reading and some were humming the verses, thus making the overall atmosphere very pious and deep.

Meera scanned every face thoroughly but could not find the one familiar face that she was searching for. She eventually stood up and went to the main prayer hall where she had first seen the little Lama.

*

Sam and Tara, meanwhile, went to a roadside café. This particular café was a popular one with the foreign tourists as the menu included assorted international snacks with different kinds of coffees and shakes. There was free wi-fi too, as an added advantage.

Sam looked around and realized that many foreigners sitting around had a hippie look and he thought to himself about how casually they dressed. His eyes stopped at a table in the corner where a couple was sitting. They had a rather dishevelled appearance.

The woman had beaded hair and was dressed in loose pajamas and *kurta*. She was scratching herself over and over and seemed anxious. Sam thought it was odd as Greg had also displayed the same behavior a few minutes ago.

He shook off the thought and turned his attention to Tara and Greg who were talking about what they liked about Dharamshala and Mcleod Ganj.

"I love the fact that people are so friendly and warm. Also the spirituality is contagious in the monasteries; I don't want to leave," Greg said, scratching his arm.

Samir turned his eyes to the itch and saw a red rash, like that of a reaction. "Do you have some sort of allergy? You keep scratching yourself," he asked, unable to stop himself from asking.

"What? Oh no, no, it's nothing," Greg replied hurriedly. "So, Samir, any favourite subjects? Which video games do you play?" he asked, turning his attention from Tara to Samir.

Samir forgot all about the scratching and the doubt in his mind and started talking about all the adventure games he had been playing online, how he wanted to travel and experience adventure sports when he was a bit older.

Greg had ordered ice cream floats for them, and he sat listening to Sam as he sipped his black coffee.

"Where do you stay here and what do you do all day?" Tara asked.

"I am staying at a guest house. I had come here to experience the spirituality of Buddhism and to understand and learn more about it. I mostly visit the big and small monasteries all day, sit and meditate there and sometimes hang out with the locals," he smiled.

"That sounds cool!" Tara said.

The three of them sat there at the roadside café, Tara and Sam with their ice cream floats and Greg with his black coffee, age and nationality no bar, just enjoying a friendly chat. Sam exchanged his number with Greg's local number and they all exchanged email ids so that they could keep in touch later.

*

Meera's search had been fruitless. She had checked the main prayer hall too and then had walked the entire compound slowly, even venturing into the side corridors but it was of no use. Disappointed and tired, she stepped out of the monastery and walked towards the café where she had left Tara and Sam with Greg.

Tara spotted Meera from a distance and knew instinctively from her pace that she had not found the little Lama. Although it was a big mission to find him, still Tara felt disappointment for Meera who had been gone for almost forty-five minutes while she herself sat in the sun, enjoying good company and an ice cream float.

Tara waved her sister to join in. Meera came and pulled a chair and sat down with a tired expression.

"Oh you look tired. It seems you have been walking instead of meditating in the monastery," Greg said.

Meera gave a weak smile "I think we should go now, Tara and Sam."

"Have something to drink first," Greg objected.

"No thank you. We are really getting late." Meera said as she got up, Tara and Sam also joined her.

Greg shook hands with the three of them and wished them good luck and asked them to keep in touch. They got out of the café and Greg saw them walk in the direction of the taxi stand.

He then took out a small, transparent, plastic bag from the inside pocket of his jacket. He looked at the quantity of the white powder inside and decided it was enough for the day as he place it back inside.

CHAPTER 11

The Missing Frenchman

Meera was quiet while walking, lost in her thoughts.

Tara was still feeling bad about letting her go on her own so she said, "Meera, drink something before we venture into the forest. We've had floats but you must be thirsty and we won't get anything to eat down at Forsyth Ganj."

"I really don't feel like it," Meera said.

"How about some veg *momos* at the same place we went to the last time. Come on *Di,* as you said we have a long day ahead of us." Sam also coaxed her.

Meera nodded her head in approval.

Sam led them to the same roof-top restaurant that they had visited during their first visit. Meera picked a table near the window overlooking the forest and Sam and Tara joined her.

Sam ordered a plate of veg *momos*, a sandwich and a soft drink for Meera.

After taking a couple of sips of cola, Meera's usual mood returned, and she asked, "So what were you both discussing with Greg?"

"Oh, nothing really, just talking about hobbies and school and he was telling us how he liked being here, the usual small talk," Tara replied with a bite of the grilled sandwich in her mouth. "He gave us his email id so that we could be in touch."

"He also loves adventure sports like I do," Sam added.

"Ya, the only difference being that he can actually go out and do all that and you can only talk about it," Tara teased him.

Meera giggled as she picked up another piece of *momo* from the plate.

"Haha, *Di,*" Sam said sarcastically.

Meera kept smiling at their banter and subconsciously kept looking into the forest, half expecting to find the Lama there.

They finished the sandwich and the *momos* in no time. Meera was sipping the last few drops of her cola and took one last glance at the forest as Tara paid the bill.

"No way! Get up guys . . . *jaldi chalo* . . ." she yelled.

"What happened?" Tara asked her.

"Look!" Meera pointed her finger towards the depth of the forest outside. Sam and Tara looked to where her finger pointed, and stared at . . . nothing.

"Look, there's that maroon robed Lama, just like the last time I saw him," Meera impatiently added.

Sam and Tara kept staring there for a few seconds.

"I can't see anyone," Sam said.

"Neither can I," Tara added.

"He's there, I'm telling you! Didn't I find that bag, following him the last time? I can see him. Both of you are not focusing enough. Let's rush to the forest."

Meera had already dashed out. Sam and Tara followed. They couldn't see anyone in the forest and it was too far for them to make out anything but they were trying to keep up with Meera who was now running towards a taxi. She gestured to them to hurry up as she got inside.

"We didn't see anyone, Meera," Tara almost shouted at her. "You are behaving erratically. I'm telling you . . . you are reading too many mystery novels!"

Meera was simply not paying attention to her anymore and kept the taxi fare in her hand. The taxi was already moving and as soon as they reached Forsyth Ganj, Meera asked the driver to stop near the church. She jumped out as soon as they stopped and paid the driver. Sam and Tara followed her to the main gate of the church. They entered but stopped at the sight before them.

*

There were about five or six policemen around and some sort of activity was going on. Tara spotted

Inspector Kumar busy giving instructions to his men in one corner.

Sam said, "Let's see what's going on here." They approached Inspector Kumar and greeted him. He turned around and recognized them almost immediately and asked "*Arre* kids, what are you doing here?"

"Nothing, we were just passing by, saw you, so came to say hello," Sam smartly hid the real intention of them being there. "What happened here, Sir? Why are there so many policemen in the area? Did you find another bag?" Sam probed.

Inspector Kumar hesitated for a moment, then said in a low voice, "We found the missing French tourist. I mean, we found his *dead* body, deep in the forest."

Sam didn't know what to ask further. Meera and Tara also felt uneasy. "Paresh, seal this entire area. Make sure nobody gets to this area till we have collected all the evidence," Inspector Kumar instructed.

'There goes our investigation!' Meera thought.

Sam and Meera exchanged glances to say that they should leave now, no point in standing around since they wouldn't be allowed to wander off. They were about to say bye to Inspector Kumar when a constable came to him with a clear bag. "Sir, we found this about ten metres from where the body was found."

There was something in it that looked familiar to Tara. She stared at it and the colour from her face drained when she recognized that it was the same necklace that she had helped Greg pick up last week.

She nudged Meera and motioned her to step back. Inspector Kumar was no longer paying attention to them. He started questioning two men who were spotted nearby.

"What?" Meera stepped back and asked Tara.

"The silver thing that you see in the evidence bag is the same necklace that Greg claims he lost. I helped him pick it up, remember?"

Sam had also stepped back and he looked worried at Tara's claim. He had really liked Greg and had made up his mind to keep in touch with him. Now he was wondering if Greg was involved in the killing of the French tourist and if he was a criminal.

"If you are sure about the necklace, we should tell Inspector Kumar about it, Tara." Meera said.

"No, I won't! He is our friend," Tara objected. "Sam, tell her. We are not going to snitch on our friend!"

Sam stood there, quietly contemplating whose side to take and what to say.

Meera continued to push her point, "If Greg is involved in this; he has to be reported. If it is just a coincidence, he can give a logical explanation and no harm will come to him. And who is to say that the necklace belongs to Greg? There would be so many necklaces like that one in the market. You are simply making an assumption that it is the same one."

Meanwhile Samir had googled 'signs of cocaine use' on his cell phone. He kept reading something on the screen and did not join the discussion.

"What are you doing, Sam? You can't be busy texting or reading a PJ right now! This is serious," Meera's temper was about to flare again at the sight of Sam engrossed in his cell phone.

Samir spoke up, "We need to tell Inspector Kumar about Greg, Tara *Di*. Greg is a drug addict!

"I noticed he was scratching his arm all the time, in fact he had a rash. He was also distracted and tired. I noticed another woman in the same café behaving exactly the same way but couldn't make the connection. Plus, he was so friendly and nice that we couldn't have thought otherwise.

"Now that you thought it was the same necklace that belongs to Greg, I googled the symptoms of cocaine use. Some of the minor symptoms are rashes, scratching and tiredness. If you remember, the white powder found in the French tourist's blue bag in this very forest was cocaine. They have now found his dead body too!

"Please, we need to tell Inspector Kumar. Greg might be involved or might be innocent but we have too many things that point out that he is somehow connected."

Tara felt uneasy and sat down on a rock. "You both go and tell him. I'm waiting here."

Meera and Sam went to Inspector Kumar who had by now directed the area to be sealed off. Sam slowly explained his observation of Greg's behavior and Tara's claim of recognizing the necklace that the police had found near the French tourist's body.

Inspector Kumar noted down Greg's contact number from Sam's cell phone, and then called his constable posted near that café where they had left him. He gave him the description of Greg and asked him to be immediately picked up.

He then called Jeet Singh, and explained to him what Sam had told him. "Your father is coming here to help us out with your information," he told Samir. "But as I need to follow up on this Greg fellow, I'll send you three to go to the *chowki* and wait for your father." Inspector Kumar said, and started walking away.

"Sir, is it OK if we go to my friend Anurag's house? It is nearby, we can wait for my father there . . . if that is fine with you." Sam said innocently.

"Where is his house?" Inspector Kumar asked.

Sam told him where it was, and since it was not far from the main road and the *chowki,* Inspector

Kumar agreed with his idea. He instructed him to call his father and tell him that they were at Anurag's house and left to go after Greg.

"And our quest for the day continues!" Sam said mischievously to Meera.

"Huh? What do you mean?" Meera asked.

"Anurag's house is also close to the forest, we can still snoop around using another path that leads to the specific places we wanted to go to. All we have to do is stay out of sight and finish before Dad comes to pick us up. We don't have much time. *Chalo jaldi*!" Sam said.

Meera patted Sam's back and asked Tara to get up and hurry. The three of them started sprinting towards Anurag's house. Sam called his father and then Anurag on the way and Meera explained to Tara what Sam had told her.

Meera felt a little better that the day could still turn in their favour.

CHAPTER 12

Anurag Joins the Team

Anurag met Sam and the girls at the main gate. "Sam, what's going on? I told Mom I'm going for a walk with you. But, at least tell me, what is this 'secret mission'?" Anurag was obviously perplexed.

Sam did not stop walking and kept his pace steady with Anurag. Tara and Meera followed them. He told Anurag about the blue backpack, Greg, and why they wanted to go back into the forest. He kept it brief and gave out only the necessary information.

Anurag was surprised but eager to help out. "I know many short cuts through this forest. You tell me exactly where you need to go and I'll take you there."

Sam looked at Meera, "So, *Di*, where do you want to start?"

"I think I want to track down the route that Chandu took from where I saw him to where he was found dead. I'm sure that spot would still have the crime scene tape. Maybe we'll find something that was missed," Meera said.

"But remember, we need to steer clear of the new crime scene. The police would be all around where they found the French tourist's dead body," Sam added.

Anurag said, "You tell me exactly where you saw this Chandu fellow. Maybe I can guess where they went from there."

"Perfect!" Sam said.

They walked up to the spot where Meera remembered spotting those three hooded men. Anurag stood there for a minute, studying the area. He scanned the ground to see if there were any signs of human footmarks so that they could follow them. Sam also followed suit and bent down. While both boys were using their basic skills of tracking, the girls also tried to do the same but couldn't figure out what they were looking for.

'I guess this has more to do with the fact that these boys have lived here all their lives and have more understanding of how to move around in the forest. They are in the trekking club after all!' Meera consoled herself at not having found anything substantial.

Tara was still lost in her thoughts about Greg and wondered if he could be really involved in all this.

Samir said, "Only these two seem likely paths, they are going towards the same direction but we would save time if we form two different groups and check for clues. We will keep in touch via cell phones and in case we spot anything interesting or if we see any police activity nearby we'll inform the other party. One group takes this small cleared path here, and the other one there."

He pointed to two different, almost invisible, side-paths. "I suggest Meera *Di* and you go together, Anurag. Tara *Di* and I will take this less prominent path.

"And let's not forget, my dad will come to pick us up in a couple of hours. We have to finish all this and be back at Anurag's house before he arrives."

Everyone nodded their heads in approval and Sam gave bottles of water, note pads and pens to Anurag and Meera.

"All the best," Tara finally piped in and they took off to a different side.

*

Anurag led the way by looking at the ground, trying to figure out any signs of foot traffic while Meera simply followed him, all the while looking for anything that would seem important to her. Anurag was too focused to ask anything and she was thankful for that. She had no idea what she was looking for!

Sam and Tara were also busy finding their way. Sam was even more focused because he had picked up the lesser-used path. Tara was paying attention only to finding clues now and was not bothered about anything else.

Meera scanned the path and the sides, hoping that something might be left behind, or might be stuck in the bushes, that would help track down the men in hoodies.

They kept walking silently for about fifteen-twenty minutes, but it was of no use. It was clear that the path was used a little, but apart from that there was nothing they could use. Meera didn't feel like asking Anurag how far they had come or to say that maybe they should turn back.

They walked for about ten minutes more when she spotted something shining in the sunlight, just a couple of feet away. It was a tiny little thing, she squinted her eyes to see what it was.

Anurag suddenly stopped and said, "*Di* we can't go further, I think the police have cordoned off this part. See!" He pointed to a yellow tape marking the area, indicating that it was not to be entered.

"This must be where they found Chandu's body," Meera said. "That means we followed the right path. I saw him there and he was found here. That means something must have happened around this area."

"This also means that we have strayed far from my house and we need to hurry before your uncle comes to get you." Anurag gently reminded her.

"Yes, let's give ourselves ten minutes to look around. Then we'll turn back and go. Meanwhile, text Sam about where we are, and ask if they are fine," Meera said.

Anurag took out his cell phone and started typing as Meera turned back to see what had been shining on the ground, just a few steps away from her. She bent down to see it was a golden bead of some sort. She picked it up and realized it was actually a coral stone and the golden bit shining was its metal base. 'This must have fallen off something . . . something golden!' Meera deduced.

She took out her handkerchief and carefully placed the coral in it. She kept looking here and there. She could make out that the grass was crushed around that path and she called Anurag to ask his opinion.

"Yes, looks like someone sat here. Little diversion from the path but not much to go by. In any case, I'll take a picture of this with my cell phone," Anurag said. "*Di* I have texted Sam that we are coming back. He replied they didn't find anything and that they are also turning back."

"Hmm . . ." Meera was still looking around and wanted some time to herself. Anurag started taking pictures and Meera asked him to take a picture of the spot where she found the coral. She looked around hard and although she could make out that there were signs of footmarks around, she did not find anything else.

"I'm done taking pictures," Anurag said.

"Time to go then! It's been almost ten minutes," Meera said, smiling.

They turned around to go back. Anurag again took the lead and Meera looked back one last time at the spot where she had found the coral. She thought she saw something else there. Something was moving, she froze and looked harder. Maroon . . . no, yellow . . . no, a smiling face . . . the LAMA!

*

"Hey, listen!" She yelled in his direction instinctively. He seemed really far because she could not make out much other than an outline moving towards her. The same serene smile and the same assuring presence! She waited for a couple of seconds. He seemed to be coming towards her.

"*Di,* please walk faster or you'll be left behind," Anurag called out.

"Anurag, wait!" Meera looked towards Anurag and almost yelled. She turned back to face the Lama and he was gone.

She desperately started looking in every direction and then suddenly saw him walking in the same direction where Anurag was going. She started running after him.

Anurag couldn't understand anything but he also ran after her. She was going in the same direction that they were supposed to follow anyway but not on the same path. She seemed to be running after something and had steered onto a fresh trail thus wading through bushes and wild foliage.

Meera was bent on not losing the little Lama this time and he was incredibly fast. Although he was not running, he waded in and out of the bushes, disappearing behind trees and suddenly re-appearing many steps further. Meera had no other thought except to get to him and couldn't even hear Anurag calling out her name and asking her to slow down.

After having chased the Lama for about fifteen minutes, she started to pant and slowed down. The Lama seemed to slow down too and turned around to make sure she was following him. Meera kept her eyes on him and resumed her pace.

Anurag had almost caught up by then and he took out his water bottle to take a sip. He was totally taken aback at Meera's unexpected run.

Five more minutes of fast running and the Lama disappeared completely. Meera looked around and realized that they were at the verge of the forest, near the clearing, and in front of the green-roofed, deserted monastery!

She looked around and yelled, "Where are you? Come out, talk to me. I'm your friend. I know you are helping us, but why won't you talk to me?"

She waited for a response but there was nothing but the footsteps of Anurag running behind her.

He ran up to her and asked, "Why were you running? If you wanted to come here, you could have simply told me. We are just ten metres from where we started our search."

"Because I didn't know that we would reach here!" she mumbled.

"What? What do you mean?" Anurag was confused and could not make any sense of this.

"Nothing! I'll explain later. Quick, call Sam and tell him to immediately join us here. I need to look around here. There is definitely a reason why are here."

Meera had already regained her composure. She took out her bottle of water, took a big sip and started looking around. She went around the monastery, found the main door locked and then started picking up the various pots and statues lying around, looking for anything out of the ordinary.

After having called Sam about their location, Anurag joined her. While setting up the Treasure

Hunt at his birthday party, Anurag had placed the last clue near the monastery, so he had a good idea of the hiding places there. They checked all the nook and crannies in the walls, checked if there was any way they could get inside the monastery but couldn't find anything.

After about ten minutes, Sam and Tara joined them and Meera finally explained why she was running and was here looking for clues. "I'm sorry, Anurag, I didn't give you any explanation. I thought you would think I was being silly about this chase but I'm sure that the little Lama is guiding me to something.

"Last time also when I followed him, we found the blue backpack with the powder. I trust my instincts completely about this and even if no one wants to believe me, it's fine," Meera said, and added the last line, just in case Tara would again get into a mood to give her a lecture about chasing an invisible Lama.

No one said anything.

"I'm with you, *Di*. Let's not waste any more time and look around." Anurag was the first one to speak.

"I'm also with you and your cookie imagination, stupid!" Tara also started to look around.

Sam smiled and started checking the windows but all seemed shut from inside.

The four of them looked for clues. But they did not find anything that could be of relevance or importance. They exhausted all possible hiding ideas and combed the monastery area thoroughly but couldn't find anything.

Meera went to one corner and looked carefully at the area surrounding the monastery.

'What were you trying to tell me, my friend?' she said to herself. She couldn't see any place that they might have overlooked and finally decided it was best to head back.

"Let us all head back guys, I think we tried all that we could."

"Hmm . . . I guess we looked everywhere," Tara said.

Sam tried one last time to see if there was any way they could enter the monastery, but he couldn't find anything.

They slowly picked up their bags and water bottles and headed towards Anurag's house.

CHAPTER 13

Long day Comes to an End

They reached Anurag's house in about ten minutes. It had been a mentally and physically exhausting day. It was only when Anurag's mother asked what they had for lunch that Tara, Meera and Sam realized that they had skipped lunch. It was almost 3:30PM by then and Uncle Jeet had still not started from office to pick them up.

The trio politely refused lunch but Anurag's mother wouldn't hear of it. She immediately went into the kitchen and with the help of her cook prepared *dal chawal* and fried some *papads* quickly, and asked the kids to wash up.

Tara and Meera were especially hesitant but when Sam seated himself at the dining table, they also joined him. The food was delicious and all the running around had made them tired by then. They ate more than usual and thanked Anurag's mother profusely.

After this late lunch, the girls helped clear the dining table and Anurag brought bowlfuls of choco-chip ice cream for dessert. They picked up their bowls and went to Anurag's room. Tara and

Meera sat in the bean bags lying in the corner. They were both lost in their experience of the day. The boys sat on Anurag's bed and Samir filled him in with the recent events and how they got involved in this case.

Anurag was surprised and excited, "Wow, guys, why didn't you tell me earlier? I really want to help you. I am well versed with the McLeod Ganj area and this forest. Keep me in the loop about the events and I can help out."

"Sure thing!" Samir said. They all sat in silence for about five minutes enjoying their ice cream before Anurag excitedly asked, "So what do we do next? Where do we go? How do we snoop around?"

Tara broke into laughter and Sam and Meera joined. Anurag also realized how he was almost jumping on his bed with excitement and he too started laughing.

Sam's cell phone started ringing simultaneously. He went out of the room to take the call because it was not possible to hear anything over the crazy laughter inside. The laughter had subsided by the time he came back to the room and he informed them that his father had started from his office and would take less than twenty minutes to reach them.

Tara collected the empty ice cream bowls and went to keep them in the sink in the kitchen.

Meera took out her hanky to wipe her hands when she suddenly realized that she had not shown the coral to the rest of the gang. She called Tara quickly and placed the coral carefully on Anurag's study table.

They all looked at it with curiosity. "It can be some clue or nothing at all *Di*," Samir finally said.

"True," Meera said.

"Maybe we should not tell anyone about this just yet. If we do, we'll also have to explain what we were doing in the forest in the first place when we should have been waiting here," Tara said in a loud tone, and hearing this logic, they all agreed that it was the best thing to do.

Anurag gave Meera a small clear pouch and Meera carefully placed the small coral in it and sealed it. She then slipped it back in her jeans pocket.

They started discussing ways to sleuth around without getting caught and decided that they would plan another outing under the pretext of a picnic with Anurag next.

"This is going to be fun," Tara said with a smile.

They were about to burst into another round of contagious laughter when Anurag's mother called them out. "Samir, your dad has come to pick you up."

They picked up their belongings and went to join him in the living room. He seemed to be in a hurry and politely declined the offer of tea.

The three thanked Anurag's mother for the delicious lunch and ice cream and she asked the girls to come back again before they went back to New Delhi. They followed Uncle Jeet out.

Uncle Jeet called Inspector Kumar once they reached the main gate. Inspector Kumar informed him that he was still in McLeod Ganj and that they could not find Greg at the café. They had been trying his cell phone but it was switched off.

"OK, keep me posted," Uncle Jeet said as he disconnected the phone.

He then turned to the kids and asked what they had been doing since morning.

"Nothing, Dad. We went to the McLeo market, then to the monastery and then we met Greg. We had plans to go to Bhagsu waterfall but we got late chatting with him so we decided to do that some other day and went to the church where we met Inspector Kumar. Rest you know what happened," Samir quickly spun a half-baked story.

'Hats off to Samir,' Tara and Meera thought. 'He has just laid down a plan for another visit to McLeod Ganj and Bhagsu.'

Uncle Jeet seemed satisfied with Samir's story and started on a report he had in his hands. He dropped them off near the house and said he had some pending work, so he would be late.

The trio walked to the house and Tara bought some chocolates for Deepa. Meera caught a glimpse of the local home-made, sweet-sour *churan* balls and bought a handful. She popped two of those into her mouth and squinted when the sour flavor melted on her tongue. Tara stared at her for a second, then couldn't control herself and snatched a few from her.

As both sisters went 'yummmmm,' and kept squinting their eyes, Sam laughed and clicked a most unflattering picture of the two.

CHAPTER 14

Uncle Jeet and the Stolen Idols

Uncle Jeet had left the kids at home and was still studying the reports that were sent to him. There had been incidents of old idols being stolen from different parts of the State and then disappearing into thin air. The targeted temples were mostly located in remote villages and the stolen idols were sometimes a century or two old. The brass Shiva idol found in Chandu's bag was in keeping with this trend.

But Uncle Jeet had suspected that it was not easy for petty thieves to move these idols in the Indian market easily without arousing suspicion. This case did not fall under his jurisdiction or role so he had shared his suspicion with his friends in the State Police Department.

Now he had with him brief reports after these thefts. Two things were common in all cases. Just before the thefts, all the areas had seen a couple of foreigners, frequenting the area. They couldn't be ruled out as tourists as they were seen a few times before the thefts, and then never seen after the thefts. Also, all the idols simply disappeared and never appeared in the Indian market to be sold.

There were a few cases of local thugs being caught in such cases but they would always take full responsibility for the theft and the cases never went further.

Now that the thieves had moved from small villages to bigger towns for theft, Uncle Jeet felt the thieves had high connections or international buyers with high connections. So he had decided to look into it and give his feedback and help to the police.

The more he read, the more he was convinced of his theory and he decided to visit a few places from where idols were stolen.

*

Next morning, Uncle Jeet left for a three-day tour. The first place he decided to visit was a town called Devgarh, about sixty kms from Dharamshala. Devgarh was primarily a temple hill-town and there were about a dozen big and small temples that housed different deities. Devotees from all across the country came here to perform elaborate *poojas* and the town was a must visit as per the 'religious tourism' list.

Two of the smaller temples in Devgarh had been broken into, in the last month itself. Ancient carved idols of Lord Ganesha and Lord Hanuman were stolen. These two temples did not have any security and the *pujaris* who slept in the temple courtyard seemed to have been drugged in both the cases.

Uncle Jeet went to both the temples one by one and realized that the temples were targeted because of two reasons; one because they were both a hundred and fifty years old, and two because the bigger temples of the same era had much more security.

He went to meet the *pujaris* in both the temples and asked them questions about what they remembered about the burglaries. According to the police records, both of them had been offered a home-cooked meal by a devotee, and not suspecting anything, they had accepted it. They didn't remember anything about the night after that. When they woke up, the temple lock was broken and the idols were missing.

Uncle Jeet's friend at the local police station also provided him with the sketch of the suspect that the *pujaris* had described. Uncle Jeet realized that the sketch looked familiar so he compared it to the picture of Chandu on his phone. He then showed the dead man's picture to both the *pujaris* and both of them recognized him as the man who had offered them the dinner on the night of the theft.

This was just the sort of information Uncle Jeet required to move ahead. He informed the State Police Department how their theft case was linked to a case of homicide in Dharamshala area. He was offered full support and documents to move ahead.

There had been another theft in Bakula, twenty kms further ahead of Devgarh, in an apparently inconsequential temple. Uncle Jeet decided to spend the night in Devgarh and move to Bakula the next morning.

*

Meanwhile back in Dharamshala, the kids were relaxing for the day, for they needed to finish their vacation homework before they took off for another 'picnic'. Deepa was happy that everyone was settled quietly at home. She loved watching cartoons, and when any of them took a break from their homework, she could explain to them the storyline of the shows.

Sam didn't pay attention to Deepa when she started explaining to him how Chota Bheem could lift such heavy things without an effort. He was just trying to catch the one side of the conversation between his mom and his dad on the phone's other end.

"Hmm, I understand! So where are you staying tonight?" his mother was asking his father.

"OK. And tomorrow morning you are going to Bakula?" she added. "Yes, the kids were at home all day; they need to finish their home-work. OK, you take care and eat properly. Bye." She disconnected the phone.

She turned to Sam and smiled, "I know you were listening in. No juicy news for you."

"Hee! Hee!" Sam laughed sheepishly, "So what is this about Bakula? Come on Mom . . . tell me please."

His mother was amused at his curiosity but did in fact tell him about the idol thefts and how the *pujaris* had recognized Chandu. She also told him that his father was going to investigate in Bakula the next day with the help of the local police.

As soon as Sam took all the information in, he jumped off the chair and walked away towards Meera's and Tara's room.

Deepa was still trying to attract his attention towards the antics of the Jaggu Bandar in Chota Bheem. "*Bhaiiyyaaa* . . ." she called after him with a disappointed expression but as soon as Chutki started laughing at Jaggu, she forgot all about Sam and got back to her show.

Sam rushed to give this new piece of information to Meera and Tara and they all sat down to take it in.

"But what was he doing in that forest then? No theft has been reported yet . . ." Tara asked what everyone was thinking.

As the evening sky became golden, Meera walked out to the verandah and strained her ears to listen to the temple *aarti*. She kept wondering about the same question.

CHAPTER 15

The Next Link in the Chain

Meera saw herself standing in the middle of nowhere and she started to panic. She looked around and all she could see was that the sun was setting and the golden rays were spreading through the dense forest. She couldn't remember how she got there and where she was going.

She tried to call out the names of Tara and Samir but nothing came out of her mouth. She started to walk aimlessly and could make out that the sun would set in a few minutes and it would become dark soon.

And just like the day before, she suddenly spotted the little Lama, smiling. 'Not again!' She could feel the frustration rising in her as she started chasing him. The sun was going down quickly and the only instinct Meera followed was to chase the little Lama and forgot about being alone in that forest without any reason.

After a chase of about ten minutes she found herself in front of the monastery with the green roof once again . . . and again the little Lama disappeared. It was getting darker by the minute and Meera could feel her heart sinking since she couldn't figure out what to do.

Suddenly the little Lama appeared near one of the protruding pillars of the monastery and Meera followed him. He seemed to vanish behind the pillar and then a moment later, one of the windows of the monastery opened. Meera peeped inside to see the Lama smiling at her.

In the darkness, Meera could only make out that he was standing in a small hall, but nothing else.

'How did he get inside, there is no opening here,' she thought.

The Lama kept smiling at her and she walked towards him. He was on the other side of the window, the window that they had checked and found shut from inside the previous day. She went towards the pillar from where the boy had vanished and started to look for an entrance. The darkness was increasing by the minute and she felt exhausted and scared to be alone. The Lama had disappeared again. She sat against the pillar and closed her eyes.

*

She woke up with a jerk as if recovering from a feeling of falling down.

Meera felt her heart beating very fast from the feeling of being alone in the forest and she moved her hands around to get an idea why she was not feeling cold. She felt the warmth and softness of her bed and was surprised.

She touched her left forearm to feel her watch and pressed the side button to check the time and look around in the light of the dial. It was 3AM and she was nicely tucked in her bed in her room. She got off the bed to make sure she was not dreaming and switched on the light. Tara was sleeping on the other side of bed and she was indeed in her own room.

'That means I was dreaming about the Lama! But it all seemed so real,' she thought.

Her heart was still beating fast and she couldn't believe that it was just a dream. She got back into the bed and poured some water from the jug on the side table and drank half a glassful of water to calm her nerves.

She then settled into a dreamless sleep.

Around the same time, in Devgarh, Uncle Jeet was trying to get some sleep before the long day ahead. He had planned to go around to the temple from where the idol of Lord Ganesha had been stolen, and show the picture of Chandu. He was hoping that he would find another break in the case.

*

Meera was reluctant to get out of the bed in the morning. She did not feel rested. But she wanted to share her dream with the rest of them. She didn't get a chance to gather everyone together till breakfast and then she casually narrated her dream.

She wanted to see their reaction before coming up with another wild theory.

"It is a sign; we have to go back there and try to look for any hidden entrance," Tara commented.

"No, it is just a dream. *Di* was thinking about all this all day so she had a dream about it, nothing more to it than that!" Sam rationalized.

Meera wanted to go herself, but kept quiet. It definitely seemed far-fetched that there could be a hidden entrance just because she had a dream about it.

"I think we can still take a look. When we go to pick up Anurag, we can take a small detour. It's not like we need to go elsewhere for this," Tara added.

"OK," Sam nodded his head, and Meera smiled.

"Is your *poha* OK?" Aunt Vimmy asked from inside the kitchen.

"It's delicious," Tara said. Their aunt joined them with their milk shakes and started asking them how much home work had been completed.

"We'll finish today," Tara said.

"Because we want to go for a picnic tomorrow," Sam added with a smile and wink.

"You want to go again? I don't like that you are going on your own. You are getting much too involved in strange incidents and I'm not comfortable sending you," Aunt Vimmy said.

"But Mom, I already told Dad the other day! We were supposed to go there on the previous trip, but we got late so we came back. Wasn't that responsible of us? And this time Anurag is also joining us," Sam argued.

"OK. I'll ask your dad first," Aunt Vimmy finished the conversation.

Deepa was throwing tantrums. She had a slight cough and was irritable, so the girls' aunt attended to her while they sat down to finish their home-work.

*

Uncle Jeet had started his day early and was already in Bakula by 11AM. He headed straight for the temple from where the idol of sitting Ganesha had been reported stolen.

He spoke to the *pujari* and asked his story of the incident. The *pujari* told him exactly the same thing that the other two *pujaris* had explained. A devotee offered him dinner and he didn't remember anything after having that dinner.

The *pujari* also recognized Chandu from the photograph but mentioned that he had seen some other man waiting in the shadows. He was sure he had seen Chandu leave with another man. But it was too dark already and he couldn't give a description of that man.

Uncle Jeet was perplexed. 'Chandu obviously stole all the idols from different parts but how do we get the next link in the chain?' This was the question in his mind as he came out of the temple.

The weather had turned a little humid and it started to drizzle by the time he and the police constable accompanying him crossed the huge courtyard and walked down the flight of stairs. There was a sudden surge in the wind and half-way through to the SUV, rain began to whip their faces.

The Scorpio was parked a few feet away so they took cover in a *chai* shop adjoining the steps. The constable immediately brought a chair for Uncle Jeet to sit on.

The rain was beating against the tin roof of the shop and realizing that it would not stop for a few more minutes, Uncle Jeet asked the *chai wala* to prepare two cups of tea for them.

He was a chatty fellow and was curious as to why there was another *bada sahib* in the temple again.

"I know this area pretty well. I had noticed foreigners roaming around before the theft too. It is easy to make out who is not from here," he went on blabbering as he lit his kerosene stove and placed an old aluminium pan on it. He added water and crushed ginger and took out two dirty looking glasses.

"Wash those properly," the constable instructed. He didn't seem to listen but did wash the glasses with soap and sponge before adding tea leaves and a generous amount of sugar and milk to the boiling water.

Uncle Jeet was not paying much attention to him and was looking at a file that had the list of temples that were targeted in the area. He had already covered Devgarh and was now in Bakula, just twenty kms away from there. The next target was a town about a hundred and twenty kms from Bakula.

According to the dates of the thefts, the thieves had targeted Devgarh first and then Bakula the next night. The next theft took place, after three nights, about hundred and twenty kms away, but the thief was caught and no other idol was recovered from him.

He did not give the name of any other person involved, so the thefts could not be linked. Uncle Jeet believed that Chandu and the other person caught were working for the same man.

'If Chandu was in Devgarh on the first night and here on the second, there are chances that he spent one day looking around or took shelter somewhere to rest.'

He took out his phone and showed the picture of Chandu to the *chai wala,* and asked him if he had seen him around.

The *chai wala* handed over the milky 'special' *chai* to Uncle Jeet and looked at the picture for a few seconds. "Yes, yes, I have seen this man. A few months back, I think. He was asking if there was a place to stay around here."

Uncle Jeet smiled, for his hunch had paid off!

The constable asked the *chai wala* where Chandu had stayed.

"There are no hotels in our town, *Sahib*, so I told him that he could go to Devgarh for the night. But he was not interested. He said he wanted to stay here only. So I told him that he could spend the night in Sohan's *dhaba*. Sohan just renovated his old *dhaba* and has built two rooms in the new one, you know, for guests. So he went there for the night."

The constable nodded his head because he knew where Sohan's *dhaba* was situated.

Uncle Jeet waited for the rain to subside so that they could move to the next clue.

CHAPTER 16

Anurag gets into Trouble

Anurag's father was an engineer with the PWD and travelled a lot. Anurag, being an only child, had the responsibility of helping his mother with the odd jobs. He was Samir's best friend and they were not just in the cricket team together but also shared a passion for trekking.

Anurag was lanky and quiet and mostly kept to himself. Samir trusted him a lot, knowing he could keep any secret.

His mother sent him to pick up some gifts that she had ordered from a shop in McLeod Ganj. Anurag resisted, because he thought he would have to decide on what to choose for his mother's friend, but gave up once he came to know everything was decided, packed and paid for.

He sat in the shared taxi and started playing Candy Crush on his cell phone. His mother always complained about his addiction to online games and his cell phone and was in fact averse to the idea of him having his own phone and number. But his father felt it was necessary, because Anurag had to run errands, and it was easier to keep in touch with him via a cell phone.

*

Anurag got off near the market and walked towards the shop his mother had told him about. The shop was in a parallel lane of the main road and only the locals or seasoned tourists visited that part of the market.

He idly looked at all the shops and the shopkeepers, locals shopping for their daily needs, and tourists haggling for good prices on the wares. There were very few domestic tourists and the foreigners there, were the ones who knew the city well or had been staying in the city for a longer period.

There were by-lanes that served as a connection to more narrow lanes running parallel. The houses were two or three storeys high with shops on the ground floor and living arrangements for families on the upper storeys. Many of these houses also offered cheap accommodation for long-term tourists who were in town for learning the nuances of Buddhism and meditation.

He was looking at all kinds of tourists walking in and out of these by-lanes while walking, when a tall, slim man crossed him, talking over the phone.

Judging from the accent, he sounded like an American. He was walking in the same direction as Anurag, so Anurag invariably followed him. He seemed to be explaining something to whoever was on the other end about his being late.

He said something about chatting with three local kids. “No, no, why would they think otherwise? I just chatted with them for a bit. Don’t be so paranoid! I’ll see you in a bit.” He disconnected the call and nodded his head as if he was irritated at the conversation.

Anurag acted on a big hunch and called Sam immediately. “Sam, how does this Greg fellow look? I mean, give me a general description. I’ll explain later!”

Though Sam was curious, he gave his description quickly. “Why, what happened?” Sam asked.

“I think the man is right here, walking ahead of me,” Anurag whispered.

“Anurag don’t do anything stupid. Let it be! If you think this man looks like Greg, I’ll call Inspector Kumar and tell him. Stay away from him, he might be dangerous. OK?” Samir knew Anurag wouldn’t let go of this, so he warned him.

“No, I won’t do anything stupid. Let me be sure. If I think it is him, I’ll call you back. Don’t call the Inspector just yet. I might be wrong,” Anurag said, and increased his pace. He wanted to cross ‘Greg’ so that he could see his face and then be sure whether or not his hunch was right. But the guy ahead of him had increased his pace and veered into a by-lane.

Anurag forgot all about his errand and followed the tall American. The American seemed to know the lanes and by-lanes too well and went from one to another without any effort. Anurag kept a steady pace behind him so as to not be noticed.

After about five minutes, he had reached the interior lanes and then seemed to have gone into one of the old houses there. Since Anurag was maintaining a safe distance, he did not really see which house he went into. He just caught a glimpse of someone running up a flight of stairs in the last house of the row.

Anurag hesitated and thought what he should do next. 'I'll just go inside the house, see what is there and then make an excuse that I'm at the wrong address and go away,' he rationalized, and started climbing the stairs.

*

It was an old, two-storeyed house and the stairway was narrow and dimly lit. The steps of the staircase were high and narrow so he had to focus hard while climbing. He could hear faint music coming from the first floor. Closer to the door, he tried to peep inside, but the light was too dim and he felt he had no choice but to get inside the room and see what would come next.

He reached the end of the staircase but before he could enter the room, he felt a hand reach out for him from behind and cover his mouth. He tried to scream but couldn't! Someone grabbed him from behind and picked him up. He couldn't move at all.

Anurag tried to kick and scream but the person holding him was strong and big and he couldn't get out of his hold despite all the effort. The man threw him into a small room on the same floor and locked him from outside.

Anurag was really scared at this sudden turn of events. 'Why didn't I listen to Sam?' he thought and suddenly realized he had the cell phone with him. He took out the cell and dialed Sam's number but couldn't get through. There was no network coverage in that room. 'That's why the man didn't bother to take my phone away,' he guessed.

He looked around, searching for a way out. It was a small, dark room with no sunlight coming inside. He switched on the torch on his cell phone to get a better idea. There was no window or any other ventilation. He could see a bulb holder but no bulb in it. The floor was old and wooden and there was no furniture in the room. The only entrance and exit was the door through which he was shoved inside.

He moved closer to the door and tried to find a gap to peep outside but there was nothing usable.

He could make out two people arguing about something on the other side of the door but the door was so heavy that he couldn't understand anything. He presumed the argument was about what to do with him.

He felt even more scared. He was in the middle of a busy market in his own hometown and yet had no way of reaching for help. He moved away from the door and started to move his cell phone in all possible directions in the hope of getting a signal.

*

Samir, meanwhile, started to worry almost as soon as he spoke to Anurag. He knew that Anurag wouldn't listen to him but decided to wait for a few minutes before he either called him or the police.

He waited for half-an-hour and dialled Anurag's number. The cell phone was out of coverage area. Samir didn't know how to take that news. 'Maybe he can't call me back because he is not in coverage area, or maybe he is in trouble, and that's why I can't get through to him.' Sam kept on thinking.

'I'll give him some more time before I inform Inspector Kumar,' he finally concluded.

*

Anurag had tried all nooks of the room to get a signal. Even if he could get a single bar, he could send a detailed text regarding his location but he didn't find any.

The arguing voices outside the room had stopped. Anurag sat down in a corner of the room thinking about what he could do next. Suddenly he heard the heavy bolt open from outside.

He tried to be brave from inside and thought this could be a chance to escape from there. He took a crouching position and got ready for the visitor. A tall man entered the room.

Anurag could only see his silhouette. The visitor seemed used to the dim light and slowly moved towards Anurag.

Anurag panicked, but on the outside put a brave face. The man had a slight waver in his walk and he stretched his hand towards Anurag.

CHAPTER 17

Uncle Jeet Investigates Some More

The man had an unstable walk. Anurag wanted to run away but the room looked so small that he knew the man would catch him by just out stretching his arm.

"Get out of here!"

Anurag was startled at this statement. He had already started imagining all sorts of things that could happen to him but this was surprising. He did not react or move.

The man said again, "Get out of here and run as fast as you can. Hurry, before anyone gets here."

Anurag did not waste any time and made it to the door. He looked at the tall man. He looked familiar but the light was still not enough to make out anything else about him.

"Thank you. Why . . . ? What's your name?" Anurag asked.

"My name is Simon. Forget why and how. Just run off. You be careful, OK? This is no place to be lurking about," he said in a hushed and tired tone.

Anurag sensed the urgency in his tone so he didn't waste any more time in getting out of the room.

He stepped out of the door, looked around in the hall and made it to the staircase that he had climbed less than an hour ago, and started climbing down. There was still that faint music, perhaps coming from the adjoining rooms. There was a smoky staleness in the house.

He got down, reached the street and took in the fresh air and bright sunlight. He looked back at the house one last time and started sprinting away from it. After he was assured that he was at a safe distance, he dialled Samir's number.

*

In Bakula, Uncle Jeet was on his way to the *dhaba*. It was barely three kms from the temple and since the driver knew where it was, they reached there in no time.

It was, as the *chai wala* had described, a renovated *dhaba* catering to the pilgrims to the temple.

Sohan, the owner, thought that the *sahib* and his driver had come to have lunch and greeted them happily. "What would you like to have, *Sahib*? I have cooked special mutton curry with rice today. Should I get that for you?"

"We have not come here to have lunch. We want to ask you about the two rooms behind your *dhaba*. We've been told that you give those rooms on rent on per day rates?" the constable asked.

"Yes, yes, *Sahib*. I renovated my *dhaba* just a few months back. Since many pilgrims come here, I thought it would be a good idea to keep two extra rooms. Although I've not had many customers for the rooms yet, but I think the business will be better during the festivals."

"We are looking for a man who had possibly stayed here. Do you recognize him?" Uncle Jeet showed him the picture on his cell phone. He hesitated at the picture of the dead man, but nodded in recognition.

"Yes, he had stayed here for two nights, *Sahib*. But that was two-three months back."

"Yes we know. What else can you tell us about him? Did you keep a record of any sort?" Uncle Jeet asked, half-expecting the answer.

"No, *Sahib.* What record? This is not a hotel," Sohan sheepishly replied. "But I do remember that he had visitors both the nights. One night it was three foreigners, and one night, two *shehri babus.* They stayed for a couple of hours and left."

"That's good information. Can you help us draw sketches of those men?" Uncle Jeet encouraged.

"It was such a long time back. But I can try," he replied.

Uncle Jeet instructed the constable to arrange for a sketch artist in the nearest *thana.*

"What else can you remember? About the movements of this man? Any conversation that you caught between him and his guests? Did he mention where he was going next?"

"*Sahib*, he didn't say where he came from and where he was going. But I suspect he was going towards Kangra. He asked me once if there were any direct buses to Kangra. And I did not listen to any of their conversations. They all just sat in his room and he bolted the room from inside. What they talked about, I don't know."

"They didn't ask for any food or tea inside?" Uncle Jeet asked.

"No they didn't. They were very business-like. Not friends. They just chatted and went. I also think he had some deal with the foreigners."

"Why?" Uncle Jeet asked.

"Because he paid with a thousand rupee note for the room and food! A crisp, new currency note. I thought it was a fake at first, because it was so new and crisp. It was not a fake but it was odd that he stayed here in a small room, if he carried such hard currency. He could've stayed in Devgarh, in a much nicer hotel." Sohan obviously had his own theories about the man.

"Hmm . . . OK. Also I would like to see the room in which he stayed. How many have stayed in that room after that man?" Uncle Jeet asked.

"You can see the room, *Sahib,* but I rented that room about five-six times after that and it was cleaned after he left. So you'll not find any . . ." his sentence just trailed off.

Uncle Jeet looked at him questioningly.

"I think I might be of some help after all," he smiled. "Chotu!!" he called out to someone.

A teenage boy who had been washing the utensils appeared by his side. "You remember that pant-shirt I gave you a few months back? You still have it or you gave it away?"

Chotu scratched his head, "I still have it. You said I could keep it but it was too big for me, so I thought I'd give it to my father, when I go to my village. But . . . . you did say it was for me . . . ."

Sohan cut him short, "*Ja Beta*, get it for these *sahibs*. Good that you didn't give it away," he said, smiling reassuringly at the boy.

Chotu went inside to fetch the clothes, looking rather woebegone as he did so.

Sohan said, "*Sahib*, I don't know how I didn't remember this before but that dead man left a pair of pants and a shirt hanging behind the door. When Chotu cleaned the room the next morning, he found it and I gave it to him. It was too big for him, so luckily he didn't use it." He was beaming now.

"That's really good news." Uncle Jeet also smiled.

Chotu brought back a pair of pants and a shirt, carefully folded and handed it over to Uncle Jeet with a reluctant look on his face. "Did you wash it

Beta, or find anything in the pockets?" Uncle Jeet asked.

"No, it was too big so I just kept it like that. I checked the pockets but there was no money in it. So I kept it like that in my box," Chotu replied.

Uncle Jeet patted his back and checked the pockets himself. The shirt pocket did not have anything in it. He checked the pants pocket and found a piece of folded paper which he placed in a clear bag. He checked the second pocket and felt a powder on his fingertips.

He looked at his fingers, smelled and tasted the powder and his face became grim. "Put both these clothing items in the evidence bag and we'll examine them more in the *thana*. Keep that piece of paper also carefully along with them."

The constable said, "Yes, Sir. And a sketch artist will reach the *thana* by evening today."

Uncle Jeet looked at Sohan and said, his tone very official, "Good! You have been of great help. Thank you so much. Police would still like to come back later and inspect that room. And we would want you to come to the *thana* in the evening to get the sketches for the foreigners done."

Sohan was happy to have been acknowledged and readily nodded his head. "Of course, *Sahib*," he said, folding his hands respectfully.

Uncle Jeet then turned to Chotu and handed him some cash. "Thank you, Chotu. I want you to buy yourself a pair of pants and a nice shirt of your size." He smiled kindly.

Chotu smiled back, hesitating to take the money, but when Uncle Jeet insisted, he took it, his face breaking into a wide smile.

Uncle Jeet left the *dhaba* with a good amount of information and a strong suspicion that the idols, and the cocaine in Chandu's pocket, were somehow connected.

CHAPTER 18

Greg confronts Anurag

Sam picked up the phone to call up Inspector Kumar and his mother's cell phone rang at the same time. Hoping that it would be Anurag, he rushed to pick it up and was indeed relieved to see Anurag's incoming call.

"Where were you? You had me worried sick. Are you OK? Was that Greg?" he asked, all in one breath.

Anurag had barely caught his own breath by then and he explained what he had experienced in the last forty minutes or so. "I am not sure if the man I was following was Greg or not, because I couldn't see his face, and unfortunately, I am not even sure if he went to the house that I was trapped in.

"All I know is there is something going on in that house with the creepy atmosphere. And why would anyone want to put a child in a dark room? Thank God for the guy who saved me and let me go."

Sam said, "Yes, thank God that he helped you. But maybe those people were just trying to scare you and meant to let you go after a while."

"I doubt that, Samir. I overheard two men arguing outside the room and I'm sure they must have been talking about me. I think this Simon person helped me on his own accord," Anurag started analyzing, once he felt that no one was following him.

He had kept walking at a steady pace and now was out in one of the main lanes and feeling confident. "I don't think we can tell anyone about this just yet, Samir. If we do, all four of us will be grounded and we won't be able to snoop around that green, abandoned monastery, like we decided."

"But this was a serious incident and we have to tell someone about it. A police raid is imperative at that house, Anurag," Samir said, in no mood to let this slide.

"Maybe we can do one thing. We should go for our sleuthing tomorrow itself and once we are out in that monastery, we will inform your father and Inspector Kumar about it. That way, we get to finish our job and the police get to raid the house too," Anurag said.

"But by tomorrow those people in the house would escape, seeing that you are no longer in captivity," Samir argued.

"It is the same thing now also. They would have discovered that I have escaped by now, Samir, and if they want they'll clear that place before the police get there," Anurag was adamant. "Please discuss it with Meera and Tara *Di* and call me back. I need to pick up my mother's shopping and head back home."

They both agreed to speak after Samir had a discussion with the girls and they disconnected the call.

*

Anurag had reached the shop from where he picked up the two big shopping bags kept ready for him and started towards the taxi stand. He was still shaken up from inside but didn't want Samir to know that. He was keen on making the trip to the green-roofed monastery too, before his misadventure was revealed because he was sure of being strongly reprimanded for the entire thing.

He had almost reached the taxi stand when someone grabbed his shoulder from behind! He was still a little nervous and this made him jump and scream. With his knees trembling, he turned around to face a tall, slim foreigner who looked vaguely familiar.

Anurag had had enough of scares for the day and he couldn't make out who it was.

"Simon?" he blurted the first name that came to his mind.

The foreigner looked aghast at the name mentioned. “How do you know Simon?” he asked.

Anurag had to think fast because this guy was obviously not Simon. “What do you want from me? I don’t know you, leave me alone,” Anurag looked around to ensure there were many people whom he could call out for help.

“My name is Greg and I wanted to ask you why you were following me earlier. I changed lanes to confirm my suspicion but I guess you got lost. Just saw you again and wanted to know why you were after me? And now you tell me, how do you know Simon?” the tall foreigner asked, his eyebrows joining together to form a menacing frown.

Anurag had begun to get a bad feeling about this so he tried a different approach. “Ohh, so *you* are Greg. My friend Sam told me about you. When I thought I saw you earlier, I followed you to talk to you. I’m sorry, I should’ve just called out for you instead of giving you the wrong impression.”

Greg’s expression softened at the mention of Sam, “Yes, you should’ve just called me instead of following me. Now, please tell me, why did you think my name was Simon?”

Anurag did not want to reveal what he had gone through, so he slowly said, “I just met a guy called Simon. He was about your height and posture. Since I saw him in dim light, I got confused.”

"Can you tell me where you met him? I have been trying to get to him for months! He is my brother!" Greg whispered.

*

Anurag was taken aback. Of all the possible scenarios, this was quite unexpected.

The expression on Greg's face was that of anxiety and he looked at Anurag expectantly as he said, "My brother, Simon, left home about a year ago for India to understand the spiritual world a bit better. Initially, he kept in touch and called home regularly, but then his calls became fewer and he would not return our calls too.

"We knew his visa term in India was over but when he still didn't return home, I started suspecting something might have happened to him so I came looking for him. I know that he is involved with drugs but I am still searching for him here and have not met him. Tell me where you saw him."

Anurag quickly nodded in approval, saying, "He was in a house very close to where I lost you. I'll take you there."

Anurag was still not sure if he should be discussing why he was following Greg in the first place so he kept quiet on that.

He looked around at the shops nearby and walked over to a store from where his mom bought her groceries. The shopkeeper recognized him so he left the two large bags with him and told him he'd return in a few minutes to get them.

Anurag and Greg ran towards the by lane and kept running till they reached the narrow lane where Anurag had lost Greg. Anurag pointed at the house where he had met Simon.

Greg said, "I walked past this house so many times, in fact I walked in the other direction when you were following me." He sounded sad. "Thank you so much! I want you to go back now. I know these people who you must have encountered are not good, so I am not getting you in any trouble. Here, take my number, I'll talk to you soon."

Greg seemed to know about the people involved more than Anurag had imagined. He took his number, wished him luck and ran back. Greg took a deep breath and entered the house.

*

Uncle Jeet reached the police station and sat down with the *Thana*-in-charge. Both of them checked the evidence clothing thoroughly and then sealed it to be sent to a forensic lab.

They then sat down with the folded piece of paper found in Chandu's pocket. It looked like a scribbled list of some sort. They studied it carefully and realized within minutes it was a list of all the temples from where the idols were stolen.

Not only did it contain the names of the three temples that Jeet Singh had been following up in the last two days, but also the mention of three more around Kangra.

"We have established the thefts from your region. And I have already recovered another idol from Chandu's room. According to this list, that'll have to be from Kangra region and two more from the same region. I remember hearing about a Buddha statue too, about a week back. The same gang seems to be involved in all the heists."

The *Thana*-in-charge nodded his head. "I'll ask the *dhaba wala* to help us with the sketches so that we can track down the whole gang. Also where are these stolen idols? We have to find out soon."

Uncle Jeet said, "I suspect they would either move the idols on the same day, before the theft is discovered; or they would lie low and hide them somewhere before moving them out of the State. Either way, we need to uncover this fast before any more thefts occur."

The *Thana*-in-charge and Uncle Jeet wished each other good luck. Uncle Jeet returned to his guest house, planning to leave early morning the next day for home.

*

Anurag had reached his house and his mother was furious at him being so late. He apologized and went to his room. He lay in his bed and tried to grasp the events of the day. He then called Samir again and filled him in about his meeting with Greg and how he was looking for his brother Simon.

Sam had already spoken to Meera and Tara about the earlier events and they all had decided to not involve the police just yet. The boys decided to arrange the 'picnic' to Bhagsu the next day and explore the forest and the green monastery one last time.

CHAPTER 19

Adventure in the Forest

Meera woke up and looked out of the bedroom window. The sky was not clear and the sun was partially hidden behind the few clouds floating around. Meera got worried that it might rain and spoil their plans.

She woke up Tara and Samir and told them to get ready before the weather played spoilsport and their big plan for the day was ruined.

Young sleuths Meera, Tara and Samir packed their backpacks with torch lights, notepads, pens, water bottles, folding umbrellas and chocolates. Aunt Vimmy insisted that they carry a picnic lunch from home but they refused, and told her they would buy something from the restaurants near the base of the trek.

Samir borrowed his mother's cell phone once again and texted Anurag that they were about to start. Deepa was down with slight fever and cold and was sleeping when they left, so she did not protest at their departure without her.

Anurag had also prepared his backpack and told his mother the same story, that they were all going for a picnic to the Bhagsu waterfall. He also charged his cell phone, kept a water bottle and a torch.

They knew they had only a few hours before they would have to inform the police about all that they had discovered in the last few days and of course they would then be reprimanded and grounded by their parents.

*

Uncle Jeet had also left from Devgarh to return to his office in Dharamshala, when he received a phone call.

"OK, are you sure about it? No, of course this case is not in my jurisdiction, but I got involved in it so investigated further. All the findings are with the *Thana*-in-charge in Devgarh. Do keep me posted on any new developments." Uncle Jeet closed his eyes to concentrate more on the impending mystery.

*

Samir led Meera and Tara to Anurag's house and they met outside the main gate. They then followed Anurag, walking quickly towards the green monastery. The sky was changing colours and the sun's rays had become cold and the chill in the breeze increased. They walked faster, knowing very well that they could be caught in the unpredictable summer rain.

Soon enough they were outside the green-roofed monastery and Meera got to work silently. She started looking carefully at the exact spot she had seen in her dream. The others also touched all nooks and crannies of the pillars and walls.

Meera tapped, knocked and pushed the small grooves on the wall section that she remembered from the dream.

She suddenly pressed against a broken section behind a pillar and heard the faint sound of a door creaking. She looked closely to find a dark passage leading from the door behind the pillar. She called out to others as she switched on her torch light and flashed the beam towards the sound.

Behind the pillar was a wooden door that had now opened, leading to a dark, narrow passage. The others joined her and they all switched on their flashlights and entered the passage with both excitement and nervousness.

They could hear the clouds thundering outside as they slowly walked in line. The passage seemed to be frequently used, as the ground was stable and firm. They reached the side room, adjoining the main prayer hall, and looked around.

Under the strong beams of the torches, they could make out that the walls were bare and uneven. This particular room must have been used for storage, for it didn't appear to be a part of the main prayer hall. The only thing in the room was an old bookshelf, placed in one corner.

They then stepped into the main prayer hall and saw the magnificence of the by-gone years. The ceiling and walls had a few remains of the mosaics of Lord Buddha and some broken furniture, but there was nothing of monetary value around.

The entire structure looked like a big, empty hall with several small windows. The young detectives moved into the four directions to look for something of significance.

Meera had found the secret passage based on a dream.

Now they were all very sure that they were supposed to find something here. Each one of them started scanning a section of the wall to look for more hidden niches or vents but the search of the main hall did not yield anything. The broken furniture too looked useless.

Meera completed her section and moved back to the back room. She checked the walls carefully and then opened the book shelf. It wobbled and she thought it would fall on her. While balancing the bookshelf, using both hands, she called out to Sam to come and help her.

Samir and Meera were trying to stabilize the book shelf when they noticed the niche on the wall behind it. They yelled for Tara and Anurag, who came running. The four of them moved the book shelf to reveal the niche.

Meera smiled with satisfaction and flashed her torch inside. It looked like a safe with no door. They kept flashing their torches inside till something gleaming in the light caught everyone's attention.

It was at the far end of the niche and one would have to climb inside to get it. Meera looked at Tara, as both the boys looked too tall to fit inside, and Tara quickly nodded in affirmation.

She climbed inside and crawled to the end while the others kept their torches directed inside.

She found two pieces of carved brass wrapped in cloth and she carried them out carefully. Anurag took the items from her hand as Meera and Sam helped her to climb out of the niche.

He removed the cloth and in his hand shone two idols; one of Lord Hanuman and other of a sitting Ganesha! All four of them knew they had uncovered a hiding place for the thieves and they looked at each other silently.

"I think we got what we came here to get! Now let's move out of here and go straight to the police with all the information that we have," Tara said.

*

"Not so fast, kids!" boomed a voice from behind them. In their concentration to retrieve the statues, they had not realized that three men had sneaked up behind them!

They jumped in surprise and turned around to face two locals and a foreigner. One of the locals had already drawn out his pistol and was pointing it menacingly at them.

They gestured to them to hand over the idols and one of the men tried to grab them from Sam.

Sam handed over the two idols and the cloth quietly and felt a small bead in his hand. He hid the bead in his palm and slid it into his jeans pocket. The men then told them to move towards the main prayer hall.

The kids had no choice but to move inside.

When the men were not looking, Meera slipped her hand inside her bag and took something out.

Once inside the main prayer hall, one of the men took out a small petromax portable lamp from his bag and lit it. The dark room was lit with a faint glow making the atmosphere even more dramatic.

Meera immediately recognized the two locals as the hooded men that she had seen a few days back with Chandu.

"You people killed Chandu!" she blurted out.

Tara gave her a 'keep your mouth shut' look, but it was too late.

The local men were surprised. "Oh, so you know more than was expected, about us. That poses a problem! Vicky, tie them up against those broken chairs in the corner," one of them said.

The local man called Vicky came into action and took out a thick nylon rope from his bag. He moved a few chairs to the centre of the hall, away from the windows. The three men then grabbed the kids and snatched their backpacks.

They started screaming at the top of their lungs but went quiet when Vicky took out his pistol again.

"We can stop this screaming right now or we can leave you here and later somebody can find and rescue you. The choice is yours!" The other local screamed above their voices.

Meera put her hand in her pocket and slowly said, "OK, we won't shout, just don't hurt anybody."

"Hmm, good!" His voice was quieter and more menacing now. Vicky took their backpacks and dumped them in one corner. Then, they demanded their cell phones. Sam and Anurag quietly complied.

The men switched off the phones and threw them aside.

The foreigner had been staring at Anurag. Anurag couldn't control himself and asked him, "Why are you staring at me?"

"Oh, you have forgotten me, *monsieur*?" he said with a smirk. "I caught you snooping around yesterday also and kept you in the dark room, didn't I? But you ran away!

"And then our man Simon went missing. I thought you just came to our hideout by mistake so I didn't do any harm but I didn't expect to find you at our meeting place too. Because of you and that idiot, Simon, we had to clear our business from that house! So what do you know about us?"

Anurag suppressed a smile, he understood that Greg must have found Simon and taken him to safety. "I don't know anything. Our friend Greg was looking for Simon, we were just helping him. That's all!" Anurag put on an innocent face.

"See, I told you that I had seen that Greg talking to these kids, when I asked him he said he was just chatting. I knew something was wrong," the foreigner growled at the local.

"So what? We had Greg do a lot of dirty work for us because we had Simon. Ideally he could have done more work for us, but after we asked him to get the drugs from your fellow Frenchman's body, he was so shaken up I thought he'll go to the police straightaway," the local said calmly.

Vicky had made the kids sit down and twisted their arms to their backs and tied them to the partially broken chairs. "Suresh, I've tied their hands to the chairs but I don't have enough rope to tie their feet too. Anyway, I've kept them away from the windows so that no one can hear them and switched off their cell phones so that no one can track them."

"That's good enough!! Let me call the boss and inform him of these nosy detectives. Then we'll also get out of here with our stash. Too bad we won't be able to use this place as our loot's hiding place or our meeting place. Hey, you are the same kids who we saw a few days back too in this area?" Suresh asked Meera.

"Yes, we saw you probably a few minutes before you killed Chandu. Why did you kill him?" Meera asked.

"Little girl, you know too much. Yes, I had to kill Chandu. He had been working solo for our boss on many thefts before but this time he wanted to keep the loot for himself. He said he had found a buyer. But we don't sell these idols you see, we exchange them for drugs! He thought he 'deserved' to keep the major portion of the earnings after having stolen for meagre amounts earlier.

"But, this extremely valuable Buddha statue was to be exchanged against a big consignment of cocaine. So, I had to kill him." Suresh said, an evil grin transforming his face and making it hideous.

Just then another person entered the hall. He looked at the kids and fixated his gaze at Meera. "You sure are a trouble maker!"

Meera looked at him and took a deep breath.

*

"Ratan!" she gasped. "But you acted all innocent and shocked the other day, when we asked you about Chandu. He was your cousin. Why did you get him killed?"

"Oh, he was not my cousin! I hired him for a string of thefts in the Devgarh area and then the Kangra area. You see, I was not shocked or sad, looking at the picture of his dead body, I was surprised about how you connected me to him?" He looked at her menacingly.

"From the fluorescent green shoes! I saw you at the cobbler's getting those distinct looking shoes fixed, and when those shoes were found with Chandu, I took my uncle to the cobbler," Meera said slowly.

"You sure are intelligent and observant. Oh, that stupid Chandu! He thought he was invincible because he never got caught even after so many thefts. I told him that walking around in those gaudy shoes would attract attention, but no, he had to have them.

"One of our foreign customers was wearing that pair and he pestered the guy till he gave them to Chandu.

"He had to dress up like a *sahib*, he wanted more money . . . ! Look what happened, we had to get rid of him and those stupid shoes caused a problem for me too! Here I am changing the M.O.

after every few thefts and there he was walking around in silly shoes."

He squinted at her, his eyes mean and hard. "What else do you know?"

"We don't know anything. It was just a coincidence that we reached you because of the shoes. But you really fooled everyone. Maintaining a low profile and not getting directly involved in any of the crimes, no one could have pointed at you.

"So you exchange the stolen idols with smuggled cocaine and then distribute it?" Meera coaxed him, to get more information.

"Boss, what do you want me to do with these kids?" Suresh interrupted.

Ratan thought for a second. "We can't leave them alive. They know our identities. Plus she came to my house with a senior officer, I'm sure the police will search for us thoroughly if these kids give them details."

Tara started sobbing and Anurag gave them a dirty look.

"We won't tell anyone. Just let us go," Samir tried pleading but to no effect.

Meera gave Tara a nudge. Tara looked at her and Meera pointed towards her tied hands. In the dim white light, Tara could see a faint gleam of Meera's Swiss knife. Meera had already cut her rope and passed the knife to Tara.

But she knew she had to keep the men engaged in talking till at least they had cut loose from the ropes.

“What exactly do you do Ratan?” she asked.

“We are talking about killing you all and you are still trying to understand what I do?” he laughed.

“Yes, please tell her, otherwise she’ll keep asking. She is like that only,” Tara added.

Samir gave the girls a puzzled look but when Tara directed her eyes towards the Swiss knife and rope, he also gained his confidence. He nudged Anurag with his elbow to make him aware of what was going on.

Outside, the thunder had brought in lightning and heavy showers. The rain pelted down hard on the broken roof.

“We’ll have to wait till the rain subsides,” the foreigner said to Ratan, and sat down on the floor. Ratan also nodded his head in affirmation.

He began addressing Meera, “I get my men to steal old valuable idols from temples that have no security. You see, not all valuable idols are protected, they are sometimes housed in old crumbling temples too.

“In fact during the string of the Devgarh thefts, I even let my foreigner friends decide which idols they wanted. Chandu did two successful thefts for me, but I gave some idiot the third job and he got caught. But he was paid well enough to not reveal the gang's identity.

"Then Chandu, Suresh and Vicky did a series of thefts here in Kangra but this time Chandu got greedy and we had to finish him off. The idol that you found in my house was from the second series of thefts and I simply passed it off as Chandu's. You did believe me easily," he winked.

Tara passed the knife to Sam as the rain outside became louder and louder. Vicky was standing near a window and looking outside at the frightful lightning.

"What do you do with the stolen idols?" Meera asked again.

"We exchange them for cocaine from our foreigner friends. The more valuable the idol is; the bigger the supply. Then, my people all around the State, distribute it to our hidden spots," Ratan said.

He looked at Alex, the foreigner, and smiled. Alex waved a thank you in return, as if accepting an award.

"What about that French man from the Tourist Home? You are involved in his death too?" Meera asked further as Sam cut himself loose and passed the knife to Anurag.

"Oh, you know about him too?" Ratan looked surprised, "He was Alex's friend and they both were working together to supply the cocaine to me. But he decided to keep a huge portion for himself. Unfortunately, he couldn't escape the city before we caught up with him and now poor Alex has lost a friend."

Alex faked a sad expression.

Anurag had almost freed himself, when Vicky said, "Boss, we should be moving. The rain has subsided a little."

"Sure but we need to take care of these kids first." Ratan said with a smile.

Anurag cut the last strand of the rope and gestured to Sam that he too was free. All four of them had kept their hands behind their backs as if they were still tied to the chairs.

*

Meera was looking at the distance between her and the petromax. She thought she would leap at the petromax and knock it down. In the darkness and confusion, they all could escape. She moved her body forward and the lightning cracked again.

In the darkness outside, Vicky saw something. "Boss, there is someone outside! I think it is a Lama. Look!" He pointed his finger frantically. Ratan, Suresh and Alex moved close to the window to peep outside.

"Bring that petromax here. I don't want any loose ends. No witnesses!" Ratan shouted.

Samir and Anurag smiled at each other and Meera gestured to Tara to be ready.

Once Vicky took the light to the window, it became pitch dark in the hall. The four of them started crawling towards the small room with the secret entrance.

"Where is the Lama, Vicky?" Suresh asked in anger. They were moving the light in all directions to see if they could also find the Lama.

As soon as Anurag reached the small room, he stood up and fumbled in the dark. But he found the secret door in a couple of seconds and opened it quietly.

The four slipped out in the dark and rain without making any noise. It all happened within a few seconds and when Ratan turned around he couldn't see anyone in the dark.

He directed Vicky to turn the petromax towards the kids. But there was nobody.

"Where did those kids go?" Ratan screamed. "Find them and kill them." He stared at the ropes lying on the floor.

*

The kids were already a few metres away in the forest by that time and Meera turned around one last time. The lightning flashed again and she caught a glimpse of the little Lama near the green-roofed monastery, looking at her and smiling. She smiled back at him just like she did when they had met for the first time in the Dalai Lama's temple.

The kids kept running at the top of their speed. They could hear the goons screaming behind them. It had started raining again and it was very dark. The path had become slippery and the rain lashed their faces and bodies but they kept running.

The men took a few seconds to see in which direction the kids had gone and they followed.

'I hope we reach my house before these men come close,' Anurag thought.

'I hope we don't get caught, for nothing will save us this time,' Tara thought.

The men were catching up fast.

Suddenly, the kids heard a loud voice from behind, "Stop running, or I'll shoot!" Suresh was very close to them.

Anurag shouted to Samir, "Let's just take different paths, Sam. Only one of them seems to have a pistol. We are not far from the house. Let's confuse them a bit."

Sam, Meera and Tara shouted, "OK!"

Anurag took the path with the maximum number of bushes. He was obviously well versed with the area and didn't want others to get lost trying to pull a stunt like this.

Sam gestured to Meera and Tara, telling them to stay together and directed them to another path that would take them right to the backyard of Sam's home.

He himself diverted a little towards the denser part of the forest. The rain was lashing against the kids as they ran in a criss-cross manner.

Their plan seemed to be working as they heard some confused screams behind them. Unfortunately, the screams were followed by gunshots.

Suresh had started firing in desperation. Meera looked at Tara. She looked pale. Meera extended her hand to her and clutched her tightly as they ran faster.

Anurag was not just battling the rain but also the bushes. He could feel his arms and face getting cut by the thorns but he kept running. Just then a bullet whooshed past him and his heart started beating even faster. But he kept running.

Sam shouted from some distance, "Is everyone OK?"

"Yessss . . . ," Anurag heard himself say that and then heard the girls say the same.

But the goons were on their heels now and Suresh was firing crazily in all directions, following the sounds of their voices.

*

"How far are you going to run?" Ratan shouted from behind. He had caught up with Samir and had grabbed him by his clothes. Samir couldn't run anymore. "I've got your friend." Ratan laughed.

Anurag, Meera and Tara slowed down. There was no point in running now. They slowly turned to face those goons. In the thunder and lightning, the four goons looked even more menacing.

Suresh pointed the gun at them.

*

They were still wondering what would happen next, when they heard a booming voice, "Drop your gun or I'll will shoot to kill!"

Samir turned around to see his dad, Inspector Kumar, a few policemen and Greg.

"Dad!!" he screamed with joy.

Suresh looked at Ratan, and then at all the policemen pointing their guns at them. They were clearly outnumbered.

He lowered his gun. He began to shake, all the arrogance out of him now, as he found himself being handcuffed.

Alex tried to make a run for it, but he slipped and fell. A policeman pulled him up, put his hands behind his back, and snapped the handcuffs on him. Alex muttered strange words in French under his breath. The policeman with him said, "It is good we don't understand what you are saying," and dragged him away.

Ratan, handcuffed too, had begun to plead his innocence already, but the policemen would have none of it.

"Take them away," said Inspector Kumar.

The four goons were arrested, and the kids took a deep, relieved breath.

CHAPTER 20

The Singh Sisters' Adventure Ends!

After Inspector Kumar took the goons into his custody and took them straightaway to the police station, Uncle Jeet took the kids to Anurag's house.

Anurag's mother had given them fresh dry *pyjama kurtas* from Anurag's wardrobe and towels to dry themselves.

The four young sleuths finally sat near the *sigree* in Anurag's living room with mugs full of hot chocolate. They were still shivering from the harrowing experience of being captured and then having escaped unharmed from the dangerous criminals.

Uncle Jeet wanted to talk to them but waited patiently for them to calm down while he had a cup of hot tea.

Anurag's mother looked worried but Uncle Jeet assured her that there was nothing to worry about anymore.

He added, "The kids have definitely acted irrationally but they have also shown a lot of courage."

The four of them stole glances at each other and smiled.

"Dad, how did you come looking for us?" Samir finally found the courage to ask the question.

"Your friend Greg came to Inspector Kumar this morning to surrender himself. He told him that his brother Simon had become addicted and fell prey to the drug peddlers in McLeod Ganj. When Greg came to India from the US, he started searching for Simon but the people who had him asked for a lot of money in return. Greg was asked to do a few illegal things for them before they agreed to release Simon.

"The Frenchman was one of the middlemen and the last consignment that he brought; he kept a part of it with himself. Alex and Greg were sent after him to coax him, but Alex killed him during a heated argument.

"As you had informed us, we found Greg's necklace at the site. But Greg was not prepared for things to get so murky and he secretly started looking for his brother so that they both could escape. He finally found him yesterday when Anurag gave him the lead.

"And this morning, he and Simon approached Inspector Kumar. Since Greg had worked with Alex, he knew the hiding place for the statues too. We were coming for the statues and had not even realized that you all were missing since you were supposed to be on a 'picnic'!" He took a deep breath and gave a very angry look to the kids.

"Sorry, Uncle Jeet," Meera said in a low voice. "We had a few leads but they were so far-fetched that we did not want to come to you till we had some clarification."

"But you should've told me about Anurag's misadventure! Do you realize what big trouble he was in? Even if he managed to escape, you had no business hiding this information."

"I'm really sorry, it's my fault," Anurag said apologetically.

"But Dad, isn't Greg an addict too? He showed all the signs," Sam said, diverting the conversation.

"He said that the gang members forced him to use the drug. I don't know how much truth lies in it but he has helped the police a lot and he plans to testify against the criminals so he'll be fine. He and his brother will be able to go back home safe and sound," Uncle Jeet clarified.

The kids were sipping their hot chocolate, and the *sigree* and conversation was making them feel better. It was still raining heavily outside and Anurag's mother had made it very clear that they all should stay on till it stopped.

Uncle Jeet's cell phone rang and he went to a corner to talk in private. When he returned, he said, "I need to go. I'll leave you all here and will send the driver to pick you later.

"Our men at the New Delhi International Airport apprehended two foreigners carrying a Buddha statue. They claim they've bought it and have some *kacha* receipt for it too but we believe it is the Buddha statue stolen from Deevar monastery.

"I hope we have enough evidence to prove it then and there and also connect it to Ratan and his gang. Guess what, Meera, they were carrying that statue in a fluorescent green bag with the 'G' insignia, just like the one you had described."

Meera began to wonder what the 'G' insignia was all about, she had ignored that till now. Well, maybe it was 'G' for Greed?

This was just another theory. Meera smiled. All her crazy theories made so much sense now, so maybe this would also hold.

She turned to her uncle and said, "I think I might be able to help with making that connection," and stood up to bring something.

"I think I can help too," Sam said, as he followed her.

Uncle Jeet gave a puzzled look and followed them to Anurag's room where they had kept their wet clothes. Meera took out a small clear bag from her jeans pocket and gave it to Uncle Jeet. It had a small coral stone in it.

"I found it near the site where Chandu's dead body was discovered," she said.

Sam took out another identical stone from his jeans pocket, "I found it in the hiding place where all the stolen idols were kept," he said.

Uncle Jeet shook his head in disbelief but didn't comment further. He took out his phone, "They've sent me a few pictures of the Buddha statue from when it was in the monastery. Let's see if the stones are the same." He showed the pictures to Meera and Sam.

Samir and Uncle Jeet compared the corals, but Meera's face had turned pale. She pointed to a framed picture in the background, her finger shaking, "Uncle Jeet, who is that little Lama in the framed photograph?"

In that old wooden frame was a picture of a smiling little Lama, no more than eight years old.

*

Uncle Jeet took a deep breath, and said, "You know that the statue originally belonged to the monastery at Deevar. There was a big earthquake in 1982 and the old monastery was partially destroyed.

"It was a flourishing monastery at that time with many young monks. Everyone escaped but they had one casualty. The dead body of this little Lama was found in the rubble clutching the Buddha. It is believed that the little Lama and Buddha statue are inseparable."

Meera gulped. Her head started spinning. Somewhere deep down, she had always believed that she was guided by a higher power but she could never have imagined that she would get to hear something like this. She sat down quietly and closed her eyes for a brief second and the smiling face of the Lama flashed before her. She immediately opened her eyes.

Sam was still looking at the picture and said with confidence, “You can connect these corals to this statue, Dad.”

Uncle Jeet was irritated at them for getting themselves in so much trouble, and did not share his enthusiasm, “I’ll deal with you all later. I need to go now.”

He walked out, then paused, looked back and smiled, “But I am proud of all of you. When we wrap this up, I want to hear all about your adventure.”

Meera and Sam also smiled back.

“Thank you!” Samir yelled and started laughing. Meera gave him a weak smile.

They went back to Anurag and Tara as Anurag’s mom brought some soup for all of them. They sat there, listening to the rain subsiding.

Tara was thinking about all the dangers that Greg had to undergo for his brother and then she looked at Meera. ‘I would’ve done the same,’ she thought.

Anurag had realized the full magnitude of the trouble he was in, the day before, and was thinking if he would do it again. 'Yes, I would,' he said to himself.

Samir was thinking how the last ten days had become a whirlwind adventure and made up his mind to join the Secret Service just like his father.

Meera wondered if the little Lama had waved his final goodbye to her, or if she would see him again. She closed her eyes and smiled. The little Lama was a part of her life now. She could never say goodbye.

* * *